COLONIAL RANGERS

MAXINE DOWN

BOOK 5

JACK MOORE

CHAPTER 1

The buzzing phone made Jessica moan in frustration as she reached out of the bed and slapped around on the nightstand. She could have opened her eyes and actually looked for her target, but the slapping did the trick and once her palm made contact the annoying sound stopped. She had barely used any muscles in that little exercise and yet it had completely wiped her out. She sighed and then mumbled, "Didn't wake you up did it?"

Jessie heard nothing so she said it louder this time and when that got no response, her other hand went searching around the sheets. She was finally forced to open her eyes and look at the empty spot on the bed. She did not have to look around for very long though. Jake came casually walking out of the bathroom while drying his head with a towel. He sounded very disinterested when he asked her, "Did you say something?"

"Never mind now," Jessie replied with a certain amount of disappointment. She fell back and tried to get comfortable before realizing something. Her eyes opened once again, and she looked over at the clock. It was late in the evening, but it was only evening. She sat back

1

up and said, "Talk about hit and run. Why are you leaving so soon?"

Jake wandered over to the sliding glass doors that led out on the balcony of the hotel. He did not bother to open them, however. He just stood on the inside and looked out at the ocean. The waters were a little churned up but as far as Jake could tell they always were on this planet. Still, with those glowing green caps, the lightening way off in the distance and flowing trees down by the South Pier Arcade it was kind of picturesque in its own way. He looked back at Jessie, very picturesque in her own way, and told her, "You know, this could be a really nice place if it had half a chance. I don't get what the problem is here."

That drew a snicker from Jessie who asked her own question in return, "You mean if everybody wasn't always trying to kill everybody else?"

Jake just shrugged and looked back out at the sea. He then mumbled, "Well it's a nice hotel at least."

Jessie slipped out of bed and walked over to him. She stopped right behind him and put her arms around his waist as she said, "I like to come down here and stay sometimes, to recharge my batteries. Being way up here on the twenty-second floor, kind of takes me away from everything."

There was an unasked question that should have followed that. Jake sensed it and her general reluctance to ask. That was why he just went ahead and told her, "I'm not going back to the station. I got a meeting I have to make. I'll be back, right after it's over with."

"I wasn't going to say anything," Jessie protested lightly as she got a better grip. Then she blew it off with, "Why would I care anyway?" Jake was not about to touch that one with a ten-foot pole. He said nothing and after a few more minutes she said, "I was just kind of hoping I could convince you to stay."

"Not too hard to do," Jake replied. Then he asked her something else, "What I don't get is, you got a nice place. Why is it we come down here anyways?"

"Oh, come on, Jake," Jessica told him, "I'm a public figure. I'm a news anchor. It wouldn't look right if people knew about us. People would be afraid to talk to me. That's how I make my living, you know?"

He turned away from the ocean and

looked her in the eye. Jake held his pleasant smile and strangely enough it was genuine. He then told her quite seriously, "And it's ok if the people that I work with know all about it?"

Jessie dropped out of the mood she was in and pulled away. She stomped back over to the bed and plopped down on its corner, "Is this going to turn in to another Barbara discussion? Again?"

Jake tossed his towel over his shoulder and began walking back towards the bathroom. He sounded quite happy as he said, "Hell no, I was just making a point, Jessie." As he went back to work in the bathroom he talked when he could, "We both have jobs to do. We're both in the same line of work."

The last comment surprised Jessie. She yelled at the bathroom, "I beg to differ, dear. Our jobs couldn't be further apart."

The comment did not seem to faze, Jake, in the least or maybe he just did not hear? Jessie chose to believe the latter until he came out of the bathroom again. This time he was buttoning up his shirt as he told her, "We're both in the information business. What we do with it might be different, but it still boils down to the same thing."

Jessie gave him a perky little smile and nodded yes when she told him, "Again, I beg to differ."

"Whatever," Jake replied.

That got a strange look from Jessie who told him, "Why is it that men always say 'whatever' when they think they've lost an argument?"

Jake struck back with, "Why is it women always say, 'nothing'?"

That caused Jessie to retreat and bite her bottom lip before saying, "Nothing."

"Look, Jessie," Jake told her as he grabbed his jacket, "it's a work thing. I can't reschedule it."

"I see," Jessie stated before she translated that for him. "Which means I am not sure I buy it." She smiled at him as he walked to the door. Then in a perky news voice she asked, "Meeting some deep cover informant in a parking lot? He has to be there at a certain time, or some gangsters are going to kill him?"

Jake actually thought about that for a

second and then he replied, "Sort of. Only it's not some gangsters that might kill him. It's his wife." Jake left the hotel room.

Jessie yelled at the door as it closed, "If you're going to lie to me at least tell a believable one!"

CHAPTER 2

The garage was pretty messy, and Jake could see how Norman Scoggins was getting away with what he told his wife, Darcy. How long his excuse of cleaning this place would last was anyone's guess. Jake's stab at a timeframe was maybe a week, two at the most. Norman on the other hand, seemed more optimistic. He kicked over a pile of stuff as he walked by it and the noise could easily be heard upstairs. That was evidenced by Darcy yelling loud enough to be heard, "You better not break nothing down there, Norm! I got my grandmother's good china down there somewhere!"

"See what I mean," Norm said with an uncharacteristic smile. When it was obvious that Jake did not, Norm quickly explained, "She gave that to our daughter eight years ago.

6

She hasn't been down here since."

Jake knocked the dust off an old half broken office chair that he promptly sat in before telling Norm, "From the looks of things, neither have you."

After tossing Jake a beer from his little refrigerator, and then taking one himself, Norm wandered over to what was probably the only tarp down here that did not have a coat of dust on it. He pulled it down and revealed the board underneath. Jake began to study all of the little circles and lines on the board. It formed a map of sorts, the kind of which you used to link things together. Jake had to admit it, he was impressed.

Jake asked Norm, "That's everything we been working on?"

"Sure is," Norm told him. "The stuff we've collected is adding up. 'Bout time we organized it so we could get a good look at the whole picture."

"We'd have done all this with computers back home," Jake noted rhetorically.

Norm did not take it that way and he told the guy from Earth, "Yeah, well Darcy is the only person with a computer in this house. The whole point of putting this down here is to keep her out of it."

Jake suspected that the real reason had less to do with Darcy and more to do with Norm's inability to use anything that required electricity and buttons. Jake tested the theory by noting, "You know, we do have computers at the station last time I checked."

That drew a facetious laugh from Norm who then pointed out, "Yeah and the reason why I'm doing this here and not out there is to keep some other people out of our business."

Jake took a stab at that, "Kent?"

Norm surprised him by saying, "Every goddamn body, Jake."

That kind of surprised Jake and at the same time it made sense as well. Jake did not want to admit it though. It was also contrary to his overall plan. He offered up to Norm, "They're good kids for the most part. Near as I can tell, Norm, that's about the only thing we got going for us."

Norm nodded and said, "I agree to a point, which is exactly why I don't want them knowing all this just yet. Jake, case you ain't figured it out," he pointed to the board and said, "that right there is enough to get you killed. What we got right here is a picture of some pretty hinky shit going on. Stuff that nobody else even knows they even need to put together."

"What?" Jake was still trying to defend his basic plan, the very plan that Norm was not so keen on. "You think one of our kids is spying on us or something?"

Norm just shook his head and sighed before replying, "Jake, you still thinking like a pro. These kids ain't. I'm not worried about them…"

Darcy's voice carried down the stairs and interrupted Norm, "What are you doing down there, Norman Scoggins?"

Quickly, Norm looked around and found what he needed. He kicked over another pile of junk and then yelled back up, "What was that, honey?"

"Nothing," his wife quipped and then Norm waited till he heard her footfalls settle in the bedroom. He breathed another sigh and this one was of relief. Then he looked back to Jake,

"Sum it up for you, them kids wouldn't know how to keep their mouths shut if somebody was trying to take a piss...."

Jake held up his hands, "I get the reference." He then pointed to the board and specifically at something he had noted while Norm was busy with his wife. Jake asked, "And what about Barbara? I see you got her on the board with some question marks. You don't trust her or something?"

Norm crossed his arms and then just truthfully let the bad news out, "More like she don't trust you, Jake."

"She just don't like me," Jake protested.

Norm just shrugged, "That too."

"Ok, whatever," Jake said in frustration. Then he thought back to his conversation with Jessica and wondered if he could take that word back. Finally, Jake just grunted out, "Why is Barbara on the board?"

"Cause she knows something she ain't telling," Norm replied.

Jake was even more frustrated now, "Like what?" Norm just nodded to the board and the lines leading to and away from Barbara. Jake then read everything around her and after that he said, "Shannon was just in the wrong place and time."

Norm was not even going to argue that point. He simply said, "And whoever tried to cut Barbara in half had nothing to do with Shannon. The kid is just an inconvenience that they don't seem to be too worried about. In fact, I'm surprised a crew like that would care about a witness period."

Jake snapped, "We know who tried to kill Barbara. That was her ex-boyfriend."

"Yeah," Norm replied, "but what I saw of that mad house kind of made me think somebody told him to do it. Don't you?" Jake did not answer. He simply stared at the board, so Norm went on, "That somebody has enough pull to scare a guy like that? Jake, that crazy mother fucker had money behind him."

Jake then thumped the board and said the name under his fingertip, "Conner O'Rouke? You think all this has something to do with mob ties? That is the guy that runs the Canadian Mafia, right? They got money."

"No way," Norm replied shaking his

head. "O'Rouke had been trying to get into Barbara's pants ever since she married his brother. Besides all that, I'm pretty sure he's dead."

Jake didn't get it, "Then why is he on the board, Norm?"

That did not draw a verbal response. Norm reached down to a cluttered table and found a file. He tossed it over to Jake. At first, Jake had half expected it to be a police report but as he examined it, he saw that this actually came from the fire department. Jake rhetorically mentioned, "Don't tell me, Tony right?"

As Jake read on, Norm scratched at his eye with his center finger and quietly replied, "You know I do know one or two people over there my own self."

Jake metaphorically exploded when he finished scanning the report, "Why didn't we hear about this? For that matter, why hasn't anybody done anything about it?"

"You in the Arch, Jake," was Norm's answer to that question. "As for the rest, does all that sound familiar to you?"

"Yeah," Jake sounded very serious, "just like the explosion that killed Roy Kingsley, you know, the day I got here. Did the city police even investigate this?"

Norm just shrugged, "Why would they? Just like Roy, there wasn't any body and, on this one, not even a car to figure out who the guy was. Assuming there was a guy. That building had repair work going on and the fire department ruled it a workplace accident."

Jake pointed at the file and asked, "You think this was... you know?"

"O'Rouke?" Norm nodded, "Makes sense. You want to move anything in the Arch, from island to island, you had to deal with one of two people."

Jake sounded very disgruntled, "Roy or Conner, right?" Norm simply nodded and that set Jake off. He got up and slapped the file down before pacing around in the limited space that the junk allowed. Jake rubbed at his chin and then he asked, "And what does all this have to do with Barbara?"

Again, Norm just shrugged, "I don't really know. I just know she's got a connection to Conner, somebody tried to kill her, and he's probably dead."

Jake stopped pacing and studied the board. He really had a hard time believing that Barbara had something to do with all of this. The only thing he could think of was that she was somehow a player and was successfully hiding things from him. Past that, if Barbara was just, well Barbara, then Jake could not conceive of a single reason why anyone would want her dead, for professional reasons anyway. If the Rangers were a threat to anyone then it was because of him and not her. Nobody had even gone out of their way to try and kill him. In fact, it almost looked to Jake like somebody was doing their best not to.

That brought about a sneer on Jake's face. He grunted and then headed for the stairs. Norm just watched him and when it was clear that Jake was on his way out the door, Norm asked him seriously, "Jake, I know Barbara is keeping secrets. Is there something you haven't bothered to tell me?"

Jake kept right on walking, "See ya later Norm."

CHAPTER 3

It was quite a different experience to have something waking you up besides the alarm on your phone, and after Tony considered it, it was also far better than a rolled up wet towel being slapped on your bare ass. This sensation was definitely more pleasant than either of those wakeups. This time it was his nose that had fired off some messages to his brain that quickly put his body in motion. He rolled right out of the rack in one of the spare barracks rooms, and let his nostrils lead the way.

When Tony reached the commissary, he did not see much of anything all that unusual. The side door that led to the porch was still open with the screen partly shut. There was a slight breeze blowing in and it was still dark outside. He could hear the distant waves crashing on the beach. All of that was as it should be.

No one but Calvin was in the commissary at the moment, and there was definitely nothing unusual about that. He was sitting at the desk he kept in here. He was wearing slippers, cut off shorts, and a dirty T shirt. It was the one he usually slept in. The guy was playing some kind

15

of video game on his computer and paid very little attention to Tony. All of it seemed as normal as ever, but what was that smell!?

Something happened on the video screen and Calvin must have gotten killed in game. He punched the pause button and then took stock of Tony. He then looked at the clock on his video screen and said, "Didn't expect you up for at least another twenty minutes. You could have gone to bed a littler earlier last night."

While the smell worked on one side of Tony's brain, Calvin's words were slowly being sorted on the other. He became slightly more awake when he realized, "Twenty minutes? It can't be that late. It's still dark outside!"

Calvin shook his head and picked up a piece of bacon from a paper plate that was sitting on his cluttered and dirty desk. Before chomping down on it he said, "you have to fly today. I hope you do remember that."

All of the words were lost on Tony. He was too busy watching Calvin chew up the bacon. Then Tony's eyes drifted down to the paper plate which was now empty but had a huge grease stain on it. Now Tony knew what that smell was. It was real food! Tony pointed at Calvin and in a semi hostile way he demanded,

"Where did you get that? Did you go to town or something?"

Calvin barely paid the comment any mind. After he licked his fingers, he turned his game back on and told Tony, "Hell, no. I got it in the kitchen. Go get you a plate. You're probably going to need it before you leave." Tony remained motionless, stunned, and his jaw was wide open. Calvin hit pause again and looked at the guy. He shrugged, "What?"

Tony shook off his shock and asked, "Did you just say kitchen? Calvin, we don't have a kitchen." Now Calvin looked at Tony like he was an idiot and pointed at the door right next to his desk. Tony's eyes drifted to the door and he pointed at it and proclaimed, "That's a broom closet. When did we get a kitchen?"

No sooner than Tony said that, the door opened. Danni Nguyen came skipping out, cheerful, fully awake, and with a plate of bacon and scrambled eggs. She poked a very stunned Tony on the arm as she walked by and said, "Morning, loser." There was nothing right about this picture to Tony. Danni had been up as late as he had. She had food, too! When did they get a kitchen?

Calvin mentioned, as if it were of no great

importance, "Glad to see one of you is awake. Too bad it isn't the pilot." He stopped playing his game and looked over to Danni who was sitting down at a table to eat. Calvin became very inquisitive, "exactly what were you two children doing down that hall last night. I heard you way up in ops."

Danni gave Calvin an evil stare and said, "You have a dirty mind, Calvin Brandt." After she took a bite of food, she realized something and then asked, "Cal, what time did you go to bed last night?"

He shrugged it off, "I didn't. I had com watch." As he got back to his game he did mention in a somewhat angry tone, "Which is what happens when a certain cheerful person swaps her job assignment with another."

Tony blinked, "When did we get a kitchen?"

Kent came walking in from the barracks door and he also looked to be in rough shape. He was a little better off than Tony, however. At least he had already had a shower and was dressed. The guy also went straight for the coffee and as he poured, he nodded to Tony who was still standing like a statue. Kent Gold told him, "Mr. Tippet. If you will not avail yourself of a good meal, may I suggest that you at least drink some coffee before we have to fly out of here this morning."

Calvin laughed at Kent and pointed to Tony as he said, "Him I expect, Gold. You though? Don't tell me, they kept you up, too?"

Danni shot Calvin a most definitive 'eat shit' look. Calvin simply smiled in return.

All the while, Kent wandered over and sat down next to Danni as he explained, "As a matter of fact, Mr. Brandt, they did. I took it upon myself last night to stay up with them."

Calvin almost fell out of his chair and he stuttered, "Wi..with… you were in the same room?"

"As a matter of fact," Kent said with a certain air of delight, "I was. We were playing cards, Mr. Brandt. I decided early last night, that if our good Mr. Tippet here was bound and determined to fly out with no sleep then the least I could do was to make sure he was sober."

Danni sneered at Cal, "Told you."

A short, semi plump, girl with frizzy brown hair, came walking out of the kitchen with a paper plate full of food. She put it in Tony's hands and then walked back in the kitchen. Tony looked down at it and then he asked, "When did we get a kitchen?"

Danni slapped her forehead, "Oh god, Tony. You don't recognize April? The girl from the…"

Tony's mind snapped into reality, "Oh, I thought I recognized her." He pointed at his plate and asked, "When did we get a kitchen?" Now that his brain was finally working, or at least it was a little faster than before, he suddenly realized a few things that had escaped him before now. The most important was how Danni was dressed. She had on thick long pants, good boots, a plaid flannel shirt, a clearly visible undershirt and a thick puffy vest. It was hardly the kind of thing one wore in the Arch where the coolest of days could break you out into a sweat.

Then Tony remembered what Calvin had said about being up all night. Danni was supposed to have been on com watch. That had practically been her exclusive job since she had been shot. Finally, Tony put it all together, "Danni, why are you going with us today? I can't haul everybody up to Valley. Even if I had enough seats, and I don't with Maxine's fat ass, we couldn't take the weight."

Danni remained quite perky, no matter how sour Tony sounded, and she wrinkled her nose at him as she said, "Don't worry. Amy's not going. I switched out with her."

Tony shivered suddenly and then suspiciously he asked her, "And does Barbara know about this?"

Danni got up from her seat and collected her trash now that she was finished eating. She remained as happy as ever, "Course she does. She approved it."

That drew a very nasty look from Tony that was directed right at Kent. He had been fully expecting it, too. He simply raised a hand and calmly told Tony, "Do not put this one on me. It was not my call, Mr. Tippet."

Calvin did not look away from his computer screen and he sounded quite distracted as he added, "He's telling you the truth, Tony. Barbara made the switch on the duty roster last night. I saw her." He then looked over his shoulder at Danni, who was dumping her plate in the trash, and with a wink he said, "It would seem that our little Miss Daniella got her badge officially back yesterday.

Good going, kiddo."

Danni gave a quick smile to Calvin but now she acted nervous and was most definitely ready to get out of here. She told everyone in a very quick way, "I got to go pack a few more things." Then she almost fled out of the room.

Tony barely noticed. He was still standing in the exact same spot that he had stopped at when he first came in. Now he was no longer so concerned about the food. He even set the plate down on Calvin's desk. Cal shrugged, picked it up, and began eating it. Tony barely noticed. Instead, he turned towards the hallway door and began to walk in that direction. He only stopped when Kent said, "I wouldn't do that if I were you, Mr. Tippet."

Surprisingly, Tony did stop. Then he looked back at Kent, "It's none of your damn business."

Cal almost got out of his seat when he realized where Tony was headed. He put his hand out, "I think Kent is right, um," Cal almost had to spit, "I still can't get used to saying that." He recovered enough to add, "Look, Barbara is flying up there, too. She's down there getting ready right now."

"What?" Tony winced in a fury, "Why didn't anybody tell me any of this?"

Kent casually mentioned, "You were playing cards."

That did not calm the situation down so Calvin took another crack at it, "Tony, the weather changed last night, we got some extra weight in the birds. I had to map out another flight plan for you guys. It's not a big deal, ok."

"No," Tony replied with a bit of anger, "that's where you're wrong, Cal. I'm the pilot. I'm supposed to be updated when something like this happens. I got the final say with anything that happens on my bird."

Kent interrupted because it was quite apparent that Tony was going to keep right on, "Mr. Brandt will not tell you so I will, Mr. Tippet. It wasn't Miss Nguyen who requested the change, it was Miss Hiller."

It felt like someone had just slugged Tony in the gut. He almost wanted to bend over. It took a second for the shock to start fading and the anger to return. Before he could have a melt-down though, a very stern voice called his name. It came from up the stairs in Operations. Tony shivered and looked at Calvin as he pointed up the stairs. The question did not have to be asked. Cal answered it, "Amy relieved me about a half hour before you came stumbling in."

Tony gulped, fought down his emotions, and then energetically took off up the staircase. That left Calvin standing around and giving Kent a very nasty look. Kent took it in stride and then pointed out, "He needed to know, Mr. Brandt. If he did not find out now, then surely he would have later."

"Yeah," Calvin snarled, "preferably much later."

"Like when?" Kent remained civil and polite, "Say when he's over the ocean piloting a helicopter? You really don't believe that Miss Nguyen is going to somehow fail to mention it, do you?" What could Calvin say to that. The exact words almost made him spit the last time that he said them, so Calvin didn't bother. He just grumbled in frustration. Kent, on the other hand, did prefer to point something out, "You know, I've never been one for profanity but in this particular case I believe it aptly applies."

Calvin huffed and said, "You mean Tony needs to pull his head out of his ass. Right?"

24

Kent raised his coffee mug as if making a toast. He stated, "Thank you for saving me the trouble. I must also say, Mr. Brandt, it does sound so much more natural coming from your lips as opposed to mine."

Calvin raised a brow to that. He thought about it. Then he finally said, "Thank you. I think."

CHAPTER 4

"You didn't tell me," came the sassy little voice with more than a hint of anger. "You think you could have told me."

Barbara looked over her shoulder to the other side of the room that she shared with her daughter. Shannon was pouting, but at least she was still packing her bag. Barbara had already been up for a while and was ready to go. Her bag was already zipped up and laying on her bed. She was already dressed in a flight suit with her thermals on under it. It was in stark contrast to the desk fan that she had blowing on her at full strength. The sun was not even up yet, and it was already too warm for normal clothing, let alone what Barbara had on. Going from the Arch to the Valley was like going from fire to ice. Once you adjusted to either it was tolerable but that in between part could be quite uncomfortable.

Barbara would have liked to have already been gone but there were just too many last-minute changes that she had to get a handle on. It irked her far more than her daughter. They knew this trip was coming. They had known since last year, and the year before that, and the one before that, simply because this was an annual mission. How could they not be ready for it!

Unfortunately for Shannon, she was close by and making herself a ready target. Barbara commented, "I wasn't aware that I had to tell you anything." Then as Barbara thought about it, she put down her pen and looked back at her child, "And besides, I thought you loved going up to Valley Station. You used to beg me to take you on these trips."

Shannon simply glared at her mother with a face that spelled out, 'And I was five.' She did not say it though. She simply locked eyes with her mother, violently threw a shirt down in her bag, zipped it up, and then stormed out of the room. Barbara was very confused, "I just don't get her sometimes."

No sooner had her child vanished out the door when another came walking in with a plate full of food. The only difference here was that Chuck was fully grown even if he acted less mature than Shannon most of the time. At least he was smiling. Barbara ignored him and went back to looking over her charts. Chuck did not return the favor. He finished swallowing some eggs and then tossed a thumb over his shoulder, "You guys are topped off and ready to go."

"Thank you, Chuck," Barbara said with no great enthusiasm.

He did not go anywhere. He simply stood there watching her. When Barbara looked back at him, he asked, "Did you get some food? Tell you what, that April chick can cook."

"Yes, I did and thank you for the update, Chuck," Barbara replied sternly. Chuck was almost six feet tall and had arms that rippled with muscles. When he was not working up at the helipad, which was most of the time, he was lifting his home-made weights. To this day, Barbara had never quite figured out why he was so into that. Nothing else about Chuck ever struck her as the health nut type. He was not overly promiscuous and despite the fact that he could easily pass for your average beach bum,

Barbara had never seen him get in the water that was not fifty yards from the old bunker he lived in.

"Do you want something, Chuck?"

Now the guy looked kind of nervous. He shuffled his feet in place. He looked at his toes. His shoulders drooped. "I know this might kind of be a bad time, Barb. It's just... well.. I talked to Henna yesterday."

Barbara gulped. She put the pen down on her papers and took a deep breath. She knew this day was coming. She tried to sound apologetic when she told him, "Chuck, look I am truly sorry, but I didn't say anything because I don't really know anything for sure."

"It's cool, Barb," Chuck told her and sounded sincere enough. He also sounded a bit hurt, "Look, I owe you everything so don't think I'm trying to pin anything on you. I know how he was and, truth be told, I kinda figured this was coming. Why do you think...?"

Barbara stood up and walked over to Chuck. She put a hand on his shoulder and told him, "You're a good-hearted person, Chuck. I do have to apologize. I should have told you when I first suspected but... I didn't want to hurt you. Not when there was a chance."

"Told you," Chuck let her know again, "no sweat. It's just…" There was something else troubling him and Barbara was not sure exactly what. She suspected but she hoped she was wrong. Then, after he composed himself, Chuck asked, "You think it had anything to do with that night? You know the one I'm talking about."

Barbara had to take a breath before she answered that question, "Yes, Chuck. I know exactly which night you're talking about. He may have been a lot of things, but I guess I owe him for that night, sort of."

Now the mechanic got confused, "I don't understand."

Barbara did not really want him to either. She just let out the breath she was holding in and tried to relax while she asked, "You haven't told anybody about that night?"

Chuck put up his hands and waved them, "Oh hey, no way. Not me. I did just what you said. You know me, Barb. I don't get too deep in things, you know?"

Barbara gave him a warm smile and a pat

on the shoulder when she told him, "I'm counting on you to keep it that way, Chuck. You know what's riding on this. Now you know a little bit more is, too."

Chuck's eyes blinked, his nose twitched, and then he suddenly had that look of revelation, "Whoa. I never thought about it like that. Are you serious?"

Barbara kept her answer short, "Very."

Shannon came back in about fifteen minutes after Chuck left. She was still in a mood, so Barbara said nothing beyond, "Take your stuff out to the commissary please." Shannon snorted, grumbled, and even hissed but at least she complied. Then Barbara finished up with the work at her desk before gathering up her own things. She turned her computer off, turned off the lights to the room, then closed the door behind her.

Before Barbara walked down the hall, she closed the outside door latch and then slapped a combination lock on it. Having to do this kind of thing seemed silly when you thought about it. The latch and lock were both stronger than the door and if somebody really wanted in then they would have no problem smashing the door to bits. Nobody seemed to realize that, for

Barbara at least it was kind of the idea. If something had happened to her then somebody would need to get in her room, and she did not want to turn it into a fortress.

As she walked down the hall towards the commissary, she noted a slightly opened door on her left. The room was darkened except for the hall lights that were shining thru the crack. It was Danni's room and Barbara could see that the girl was sitting in there on her rack in the dark doing absolutely nothing at all. Barbara thought it was kind of strange but far from the strangest thing she'd seen around here. She pushed the door a little more open until she could see the young girl's face. Barbara then told her in a motherly kind of way, "Get your things, sweetheart. We need to get going."

It seemed like it took Danni a few moments before she even realized that she was being spoken to. When she finally did acknowledge Barbara's presence, Danni simply looked up and formed a smile. After another few seconds she said, "Yeah. I'm ready."

Barbara wondered about that, "Are you?"

Danni blinked and then she stood up. She seemed cheerful and her usual self, "Yeah. I

31

told you that last night. I've been ready. Thank you for reinstating me. I know that…"

Barbara did not have time for this right now. She simply raised her hand and told the girl, "Not now, Danni. Like I said, you came thru during that whole PBS thing. You earned it so get your bags and let's get moving." As Barbara began walking, she noted that Danni looked almost frozen in place. Barbara stopped at the commissary door and looked back down the hall. Finally, the girl came out with her bags and seemed normal enough. Barbara simply shrugged and turned to enter the commissary.

Barbara walked right into Jake who was headed in the other direction. He was also yawning and rubbing his eyes. The entire situation resulted in a collision. Barbara snapped at him, "Will you watch where you're going!" Jake seemed to have barely even registered what happened as he finished his yawn. Barbara had to pick up the bag that she dropped. She was angry and he was numb. Then Barbara wondered, "What are you doing up so early? You're not going."

Jake stretched a little and said, "Going where?" Then he slapped his face and continued, "Oh, yeah. You're going up to Valley today. What was that for again?"

Barbara pushed him aside as she continued into the commissary. She told him as she did, "Vaccine run, you know? I sent you a memo."

"Oh," Jake looked confused, "those emails you keep sending my phone. I put them all in a special folder. I plan on getting around to reading them one day."

Right then, Danni also pushed her way past Jake. She smiled and playfully poked him in the chest as she did. She also gave Jake a perky little, "Morning, sleepy head." Unlike Barbara who had stopped at Calvin's desk, Danni walked right out the screen door. Jake just stood there for a moment and when he was sufficiently convinced that Barbara was going to continue ignoring him, he figured to count his lucky stars and head for his room.

After Barbara heard a door shut, presumably Jake's, she stopped discussing business with Calvin and looked to the hallway. She then asked Brandt, "How long has he been up?"

Calvin simply shrugged, "How should I know? He just got here."

That made Barbara wonder. She was normally asleep at this time of the morning. If he was going to stay out all night, then why would he come wandering in so early? She dismissed the question for now and then asked Cal, "Everybody else head for the pad?"

Cal tossed a thumb towards the screen door, "Out in the parking lot. Chuck's standing by and waiting to drive you all up there."

Barbara was almost afraid to ask the next question, "Tony?"

Cal was afraid to answer, "He's Tony." That caused Barbara to sigh in frustration and then Cal added, "I think he was a little miffed about two flights going up this year. It almost wounded his personal honor. Like you don't trust him or something."

Barbara knew two things about that. The first was that they did not have any choice in the matter. They were carrying a lot more vaccine this year. It was not a great deal more, but it was enough. They had been pushing the range of their birds with the normal amount. What they had loaded up now had increased the weight which subsequently decreased the range of her birds beyond the limit of what Barbara judged as safe. The second part was that she knew his attitude had very little to do with anything as trivial as crashing in the ocean due to lack of fuel.

Cal did point out in Tony's defense, "You know, he does kind of have a point, Barbara. I'm not so sure that extra vaccine is even worth the bother. It's not like those people are going to take it."

"That is not our concern, Cal," Barbara replied as her eyes focused on the stairway to ops. She then noted, "And I don't think it's Tony's either." That was not a subject that Calvin was even willing to touch right now. He saw where Barbara was looking, he knew who was up there and he understood exactly what she meant. Of course, Cal did not have to say it since Barbara did it for him, "And I am getting sick of their bullshit."

CHAPTER 5

The sun had finally made it clearly above the horizon and Amy knew what that meant for her. Cal had gone to bed some time ago and for the next few hours at least, it meant tranquility.

She could get a few things done. Sadly, as she was well aware of the good side of that tranquility came to its inevitable conclusion when she heard a car door slam. Amy walked over to the windows that were facing the parking lot. She could not see much since no one had bothered to trim the tree branches that now obstructed most of their sandy lot. She saw enough though. She sighed in frustration.

It just figured that the first person to get in this morning would be the bouncy little set of sneakers, attached to the bare set of legs, that were currently skipping across the sand towards the building. Amy grunted and wondered if she was going to survive this day. She wandered back over to her chair, sat down, and then checked the status of the choppers. They were almost halfway to the continent and everything looked fine. The flight was shaping up to be uneventful and Amy only wished that her day would be the same. She knew better.

The sounds of footfalls on the staircase even sounded perky. The girl with the short blond hair, even shorter cut offs, and a green stripped tank top just oozed energy as she reached the floor of operations. She was also a bit distracted. She was busy typing away on her phone as she walked over to another chair, took a seat, and stretched her legs up on a countertop. She also happily mumbled with a cute little smile, "Morning, Red."

Amy did not bother to look at the girl. All she said in reply was, "Leslie."

If Leslie took any notice of the lack of a response, then she gave no hint. She kept right on with her typed conversation as she engaged Amy in the verbal, "I see that April is here. Does that mean there is some real food downstairs?"

Amy still looked out at the ocean and replied, "Probably."

This time Leslie looked up from her screen and took note of the redhead who appeared to be somewhere other than the chair that she was sitting in. Leslie decided to tell the girl, "You know, Ricky has been bugging the shit out of me all morning. I think he's got the hots for that little Shannon. He can't reach her and guess who he's asking why?"

Amy still did not even attempt to make eye contact, "She's flying up to Valley this morning."

Leslie happily thought about it and said, "Do I tell him that?" After some more consideration she said, "No, he's pouting like a sorry little cocksucker." Then a lightbulb went on and she gleefully announced, "That's what I'm going to tell him!"

Finally, Amy looked at the girl and she sounded a little bit miffed when she asked, "Are you going to be like this all day?"

Leslie tossed her phone aside for the moment and then crossed her arms. She seriously asked, "I think I might need to be the one asking that question. I don't get you, Amy. You risked your life to jump in the drink to save mine." Leslie stood up and as she did, she pointed out, "Which was stupid by the way." Then as she walked past Amy and started randomly thumping computer screens as she continued, "And ever since, you have been acting like you want to throw me right back in. What gives?"

Amy huffed, crossed her arms, and then practically demanded, "Would you stop touching things!"

Leslie leaned up against the counter, crossed her own arms, gave a smug smile and replied, "Why is it I get the feeling that touching things is what this is really all about? I got put up here today so that you could show me what to touch and what not to. The only problem seems to be that you don't want to touch anything here." Leslie motioned to the computer screens, "But you don't seem to want anybody else to either."

Amy's eyes bulged, "That's not true."

Leslie did not buy it for one minute and she became even giddier, "Yeah, sister, well I don't know how to fly so I don't think I'll be touching any pilot's stick anytime soon. So why don't you just lighten the hell up and show me how all this stuff works."

The anger that Amy was feeling began to diminish as she became more confused. She suddenly went into meek mode and cautiously raised a finger as she asked, "Wait a minute, are you saying what I think you're saying?"

Leslie dropped the giddy and sighed in frustration, "I'm not saying anything, Amy. What I'm trying to get across is the last thing I want to do is be stuck up here all day with a stick in the mud."

The devil must have heard because the next set of footfalls on the stairs sounded particularly angry. Before Amy even saw who was making the noise she said, "Good morning,

Norm."

Norm had no such greeting to give. He simply walked past the two girls and asked, "Did Calvin get my files last night?"

Amy just rolled her eyes, since she expected as much, and then pointed to the bin over by the printer, "Yeah and I printed them out. Are you adding on to your house or something?"

Norm was busy scanning the papers and barely heard the question. After a moment he snapped back into reality and told Amy, "Yeah something like that. Is Jake up yet?"

Amy gritted her teeth and shrugged at the question before she finally admitted in a long exhale, "I seriously doubt it. He didn't get in till after I was already here." Norm only replied with an evil stare that made Amy even more self-conscious than usual. She meekly sniffed out, "Sorry?"

Norm rolled up his papers in an agitated kind of way and then walked for the stairs. Once they heard him reach the commissary, Leslie looked to the redhead and asked, "Is it always like this around here in the mornings?"

Amy only groaned, "Pretty much."

Down the stairs, in the back hallway, the pounding on the door echoed throughout the barracks. The first person to respond was Calvin. He yelled out from behind his own door, "I'm trying to sleep, Norm!"

When Jake opened his door, the one that Norm had been beating on, he was easy going. He had also obviously just gotten out of the shower and changed his clothes. He was still drying what was left of his hair with a towel and as Norm entered the room and shut the door behind him. Then he told Jake, "Heard tell you was out all night."

"Sure was," Jake said without much fanfare. He kept right on with his business and paid Norm very little attention.

Norm crossed his arms and examined Jake carefully. He then huffed out, "You look awake enough."

"Just cause I wasn't here didn't mean I wasn't sleeping," Jake replied as he tossed his towel aside.

Norm simply nodded and told him, "Fine, get your ass ready. We got something to take

41

care of."

Jake shoved his phone in his pocket and then said, "That much is true. WE do have something. Only thing is, the stuff we got to do are two separate things today."

Norm huffed and glanced down at the papers in his pocket. He controlled his temper and then asked, "What's that supposed to mean?"

"Come on, Norm," Jake shot back, "It's called division of labor. I know what you're looking for and you don't need me. Meanwhile I do have something else that needs to be done. I think it's just as critical."

"Care to inform me as to what," Norm asked in a gruff manner.

"No, I don't," Jake told him. When Jake did not get a response, he stopped what he was doing and looked at Norm. He explained, "It's better if you don't know."

"Really," Norm sounded unconvinced, "Who you really trying to keep this from, Jake?"

"Who do you think?"

There was only one answer to that question. Norm just sighed and told him, "Look if this about what we talked about last night…"

Interrupting him Jake said, "We talked about a lot of things last night, Norm. I've had some time to think about it since then. You made some valid points and they have to be dealt with before we can go any further."

"Like what?" Norm burst out with. He was obviously not that happy about it either.

Jake mulled over that before replying, "Oh like this is getting a little bit out of hand. Come on, Norm, you of all people know what's on that board in your garage. You probably look at that thing every spare second. You know how much shit that is? I don't even mean how dangerous. I just mean how much."

"So," Norm shrugged it off, "I dealt with plenty of complicated cases when I worked for the city."

Jake's eyes narrowed, "Not like this you didn't."

"They're a bunch of serial killers, Jake," Norm replied. "When you boil it down, that's all they really are."

"And that's where you're wrong, Norm," Jake told him as he got back to finishing his business, "They're not serial killers. They're professional killers. There is a very distinct difference."

"Ok, fine," Norm gave in before pointing out, "They're serial killers who found somebody to pay them to do it."

"Not even that," Jake told him. "They aren't killing people because they think it's fun, Norm. They're doing it because it's a means to an end. They didn't attack us because it was emotionally gratifying. They don't even have emotions to gratify. Pulling a trigger to these guys ain't no different than somebody else flipping a Foo King burger on a grill."

Norm nodded since he didn't particularly disagree on any point. He just didn't like these people, so he wasn't going to give them any credit at all. Murder was murder as far as he was concerned. The only reason that the question of why they did it was important at all was, "And that's the good news, Jake. It makes them predictable. It means there's a logic behind what they do."

"You don't get it," Jake said shaking his head. He took a moment to compose his thoughts and then he said, "Look, Norm, I know you knew everything I just said. You're a good cop." Jake considered that for a minute and then added, "Course I never really known all that many so take as much out of that as you want. Not the point though. No offense but these guys they are way out of your league too."

Norm bluntly stated, "I've handled some contract killers in my day."

"Sure, you have," Jake told him. "That's amateur night, Norm. You're talking about a guy that gets a name on a piece of paper and then jumps his target the first opportunity he gets."

Norm sounded unconvinced, "And that's not what these guys are doing?"

"No, they aren't," Jake stated resolutely. "These kinds of guys, they don't wait for opportunities. They create them. These guys are proactive, and they are taught how to come at you from directions you didn't even know were there. They'll blindside you and when it's all over with you won't even know it was them that did it. They're not looking for credit. They're not even going to boast about it over beers to each other. The only thing they care about is the objective."

Norm still remained unconvinced, "And what is that exactly?"

Jake admitted, "I don't know. We're not dealing with the B team here Norm. The first thing they're going to do is make sure nobody can figure that out."

"You know, Jake," Norm replied in a very observant way, "you know a hell of a lot about how they operate."

"What?" Jake sounded like that was the stupidest thing he had ever heard, "Of course I do, Norman. You know what my background is."

"Yeah, I do," Norm simply grabbed the door handle after he decided he was wasting his time here. As he left, he simply said, "Good luck with your little project." The tone came off as a definitively angry insult. It was not that disturbing to Jake since almost everything that Norm said sounded that way.

Jake simply finished up and then waited a few more minutes. He stuck his head out the door and when it seemed as if the back end of the building was silent and dead, he left his room. Jake did not walk down to the commissary door. He walked in the opposite direction to the very back of the barracks. He stopped in front of the door to Barbara and Shannon's room. He looked at the combination lock on the door and he flipped it with a grunt of frustration as he mumbled, "Damnit, Barbara. What do you think you're doing?"

CHAPTER 6

It had been something of an old question. Kent slipped out of the chopper door and into the wet grass which was about the closest that Valley Point Air came to having its own heliport. He looked up into the sky but all he really saw were clouds and distant mountains. The airport's main terminal was down past the runway but there was little else here. Kent looked back at the chopper and as Barbara and Shannon were climbing out, he put the question to them, "Where is Mr. Tippet?"

Shannon seemed a little less irate than when the journey first began. Kent had expected as much since he doubted anyone's capacity for holding a grudge across the better part of an exhausting day long helicopter ride. By the time that they were halfway here nobody had the energy to hold a conversation. Still, Shannon showed that she had not forgotten anything. Her very first act from the time that her feet hit the ground was to pull out her phone and see if she had any reception. Predictably she did not, and it was something that Kent could have told the girl if she had just asked. For that matter, Shannon should have known anyway.

The girl only grunted in frustration. She sneered at her phone and then at her mother. She then snapped, "My life is over!" Then she stomped off.

As Barbara finished pulling off her gloves, she stopped next to Kent and then took her own good look at the sky. As she did, Barbara seriously had to ask, "What has gotten into her?"

Kent had to think that matter through and carefully. He finally just decided to say, "You know how that is, Barbara. She's just reaching that age."

Why was it that this perfectly obvious revelation did not make Barbara feel better? She also knew a dodge when she heard one, but it was not an issue she wished to take up with Kent. She looked back over to where Shannon had stomped off to. There was a wire fence that ran along this part of the airfield and just to the other side was a grazing pasture for a small herd of horses. Shannon had climbed up on the fence and was trying to coax one to come to her. She'd been doing that since the first time Barbara and Ian had brought her up here. As Barbara watched the child do it now, she felt almost like nothing had ever changed. Instead of being comforting though, it only seemed to highlight how much really had.

Barbara decided to change the subject and then checked the time on her phone before saying, "Tony said he had picked something up on the emergency band. He said he would be a little late."

"Ah," Kent nodded, "is that what it was."

The look that Barbara saw in the man's face told her, "What do you think it is, Kent?" He merely smiled and shrugged so Barbara got down to cases with him, "What was I supposed to do? I can't put you two in the same chopper for an extended flight. As I recall, you almost got in a knock down drag out with him not long ago."

"I said nothing." Kent replied feigning innocence before pointing out, "and as long as you are clear on the fact that Mr. Tippet and I quite often disagree, well on this matter I happen to think he is right. It would have been a lot better if you had left the duty roster alone."

Barbara gave the man an evil eye and put her hands on her hips, "You really think it would have been any better if I had shoved Amy in that chopper instead of Danni?" Barbara just shook her head and went back to looking for her missing helicopter. As she watched the sky, she mentioned, "Come on, Kent, I thought you were smarter than that."

"Oh, I'm not disagreeing with that part of it, Barbara," he told her. Then he added, "I just think that I should point out that there are other considerations to this matter that quite possibly you may have overlooked."

"Yeah?" She was obviously unconvinced, "Like what?"

"Well," Kent thought about the matter and was doing his best to juggle around the subject till Barbara called him on his indecision. He finally just said, "This is a medical mission after all. Wouldn't it be prudent if we had both of our...?"

Barbara rolled her eyes at him, "Don't bullshit me, Kent. Just spit it out."

"All right, fine," Kent tried another branch to offer. "Splitting up Tippet and Hiller was probably a good idea. I just think that replacing her with Nguyen might not have made the situation any better. That's all."

Barbara thought about that for a second and became a bit more cautious, "What's wrong with Danni? I think she's learned her lesson and..."

"No," Kent waved a hand. He tried to be tactful now, "Don't get me wrong, Barbara. I really do believe you were a more than worthy successor to your father. You just sometimes don't quite see what's right in front of you."

"English, Kent," Barbara demanded.

"Really?" Kent just looked in her eyes and wondered if there was even a spark of recognition. He did not see any, "You haven't noticed the way that our little Miss Daniella looks at Agent Tippet?"

Barbara nearly slapped her forehead and

she moaned in pain, "You have got to be kidding me!"

"Believe me, Barbara," Kent told her, "I wish I were. I probably would have never even brought this up, it's really none of my business. It just finally occurred to me that you really don't know."

Barbara growled, "What is it with Tony?"

"I'm not sure I would blame him," Kent replied.

"Yeah," Barbara made it plain that she was not convinced of that, "Well I am."

"And," Kent told her, "that is your motherly instincts kicking in. You have to look past that, Barbara, at least here. Mr. Tippet is a reasonably attractive male with at least some redeeming qualities."

"Give me a break, Kent," Barbara blew the suggestion off. "He's a big kid. He's got that whole bad boy thing going for him and..."

"You mean like Ian," Kent told her.

Barbara almost bit his head off but at the

last second, she pulled back. Then she looked back towards the sky and said, "I'm sure they'll be here any minute."

It was more than a few minutes. Killian Rayne and his little crew had already driven up, loaded the vaccines from Barbara's chopper into the beds of their pickup trucks, and were sitting around on the tailgates when they first heard the blades of Tony's chopper. Barbara found that she did not mind waiting as much as she thought she might have. Killian was the local law here at the Valley Point settlement and was probably one of the more unusual sheriffs here on the continent. He was younger than one might think, relatively fit, and had dark hair with a beard to match. Barbara also found that he could be quite entertaining when he wanted to be.

They all sat around and listened to his stories and he even made Shannon forget all about whatever she had been sulking over. When Rayne heard the distant chopper, he slapped one of the crates behind him and quickly finished his latest story. He told Shannon directly, "Actually we call this Maxine because of your Mom."

Shannon giggled and looked to Barbara as she exclaimed, "No way!"

Barbara put her hand over her face that had turned a light shade of red, "Don't you dare, Killian."

Kent egged things on, "I've heard several versions of this story already. It might be quite entertaining to hear the sheriff's version of events."

It was clear that Killian was going to go on no matter what. He was always quite animated as he told the stories, "Your mother was up there at about fifty thousand feet…"

Barbara had a smile as she angrily protested, "I never fly that high."

Killian kept right on, "Terrible bloody cross wind. She was flying right through this storm. If you don't believe me ask Lucy, she was in the tower that night."

Barbara protested, "Lucy was in high school when that happened!"

Killian shrugged it off, "She worked after school. Anyway…"

Once again Barbara injected, "After school, huh? You were just telling us it was at

54

night, Killian."

"Which is," he gracefully replied, "after school. Anyway, without further interruptions, the pattern is full, and your mother is low on gas. Well she had so much cargo and she is so short after all," Killian then looked Barbara in the eye and said, "Which does not diminish your beauty in any way, my dear. She was actually sitting on a crate of medicine. She tries to stress the urgency of her situation and the importance of her mission. So, she tells the tower what she is carrying and where."

Shannon looked so excited, but she really didn't get it and she said as much. Then Killian tells her, "Which is why poor Lucy was so confused about your mother who was riding in Maxine."

Shannon winced, "Eww, why did she say that?"

Kent snickered, "She didn't, dear. That's what the word vaccine sounds like on the radio."

Barbara rolled her eyes, "And that story isn't even close to being true." She saw her other chopper approaching the field and was relieved. She was also surprised that they had plenty of daylight left to do the unloading. There was not enough time to fly up to their station, but Barbara was also not in much of a hurry to do so. She waited a safe distance till the rotors stopped spinning and was a bit curious when she saw Danni get out of the chopper and run right up to her. The girl seemed pretty happy and that normally would have made Barbara feel better. This time it did not.

Fortunately, what Danni began to blabber on about had little to do with Tony, who joined them a few moments later. Unfortunately, just because Barbara knew what everything was not about did not mean that she knew what it was. Barbara looked to Tony, who seemed a bit more rational, and surprisingly even tempered at the moment, so Barbara then asked him, "What is she talking about?"

Now it was Tony's turn to be confused, "You're not mad at me for being late?" When Barbara did not respond he gave her an "Oh well" kind of look and then translated Danni's excitement, "When we were making the hump...."

Barbara put her hands up, "Let's skip to the chase."

Killian and his crew wandered by right then so that they could start unloading the chopper. Naturally, Killian heard what was said. Surprisingly, the only comment he made was when he grabbed Tony's hand and shook, giving the boy a most eager, "Congratulations on your execution of a most difficult maneuver, Mr. Tippet." He then gave Danni a sly look and even winked as he said, "Lovely Daniella."

Danni winked back and said, "Hey, Kill." When he walked off to join his crew Danni became confused, "What was that all about?"

Shannon and Kent came walking up and at that point it was the teenager who pointed out, "I think it had something to do with the hump."

Barbara was starting to feel her blood pressure going up again, "Tony! Just tell me what happened. Why were you even crossing the mountains that far north?"

Danni became excited and jumpy, "I wanted to see the waterfalls at Westridge."

Before Barbara could blow up at them, Tony quickly got to business, "We had to pick up some altitude coming off the slope and when I got high enough, we kept getting these

57

intermittent pings off some transponder."

Barbara knew a distraction when she heard one but, in this case, Tony pulled it off. She became very curious and did not jump on them for being stupid enough to alter their flight plan like that. Barbara thought about it for a minute and then she looked to Kent, "What's that far out from the river?"

After thinking about it for a minute Kent replied, "Nothing that I'm really aware of. I think Benthic used to have some mining camps out there, but they haven't been used in years. Certainly not since the war."

Danni was still excited, "We thought it might be a downed plane or something, you know, like a small civilian aircraft."

"Always possible," Kent noted. "There are a lot of bush pilots out here. Hardly any of them ever file flight plans."

That made Barbara think harder and she looked back to Tony, "What did it sound like to you?"

Tony shoved a stick of gum in his mouth and found himself nudged by Danni until he had to hand over his pack. Then he told

Barbara, "I don't know. It was pretty weak. We tried to get a fix on it, that's what took so long. Couldn't manage it though."

At that moment, Barbara decided that they had enough on their hands. She also decided not to put herself in any more stressful situations, or at least not for the moment. She snapped her fingers until she had every one's attention, "It's for later. It's too late to fly on up to the station. We're going to stay here for the night. In the morning, I'll get a list of any recently missing aircraft. Then maybe we can pull out some gear that can help us track it down. I'm sure the Rayne's have something. Tony, you did mark the location on your charts, right?"

"Course," Tony replied as if he were offended.

"Good," Barbara replied with a half-relieved look. Then she took a good look at Danni. The girl barely even noticed the fact that she was being studied. It made Barbara feel frustrated all over again.

This fact was not lost on Kent. He noticed that Barbara was looking at Danni, who was in turn looking at Tony, who seemed to be completely oblivious to all of it. At least the last part was a small blessing. Kent spoke up and tried to offer a solution to Barbara's distress, "I was thinking that I might stay on in Valley Point. I need to discuss some matters with Dr. Dykstra before we have to deal with that little added difficulty. I do not believe that should be done alone. I was thinking Miss Nguyen could assist me in the matter."

Danni quickly became irate, "No way in hell, Kent. I just got out of detention. I'm not going to sit in the corner now, not when we got a possible crash site out there."

Barbara raised her hands, "Let's just go get some rooms. We'll talk about this in the morning. I know everybody needs some sleep." Barbara took one more good look at Danni and Tony. Then she put her hand on Danni and said, "Come on. I know Lucy has got an extra bunk."

Tony wanted to protest, "You know, we did have some…"

As Barbra was walking off, with Shannon and Danni in tow, she did not even bother looking back when she commanded, "Rack time."

CHAPTER 7

It was somewhat disturbing to see the face that showed up on the video monitor. Barbara leaned back in the chair for a moment as the girl on the screen rattled on in her usual manner. Before Barbara said anything, she looked around the room that everyone here routinely called 'the tower.' Some seventeen-year old boy was sweeping up but past that no one else was in here at the moment.

Barbara had no idea why they called this place a tower since it was really just one more building on the property. It did actually have windows that looked out on the main runway and computer screens that handled the air traffic control for the airspace around Valley Point. After that, the place shared no resemblance to anything that could be remotely described as a tower. If Barbara had ever been forced to describe this place, the word tower would not be it. To her, it looked more like a cheap building on the set of an old western movie.

The look was just skin deep. The tower

did have a more than adequate electronics suite and that was why she was here. There were no wireless cell communications on the continent. If you wanted to talk to someone you needed either a hardwired line or a very expensive dish that could connect you to an even more expensive satellite relay. Since no hardwired lines ran to the Arch, Barbara was stuck going the satellite route to place this call.

"April," Barbara said for about the third time, "this call is expensive, please!" That really confused the girl and she thankfully stopped talking. Barbara took the pause and said, "Who is supposed to be up there?" Then the thought crossed Barbara's mind, 'Why was April in Ops in the first place?'

Fortunately, April never got a chance to explain. Amy's face showed up on the screen and it was obvious that she did not realize how much of a picture was being transmitted. Barbara watched Amy push April out of the way and sit down in the vacated chair. Amy looked flustered and told Barbara in her meek tone, "Sorry, had to go…" Her eyes drifted to the side of the room and Barbara guessed that Amy was looking at the bathroom door.

It was irrelevant so Barbara stopped the girl and just asked, "Just fill me in, Amy."

Amy looked confused, "On what?"

"Um," Barbara dropped her head and shook it, "on anything? It's my station you know. I do like to keep up with what's going on."

Amy just looked around the room on her end, like she might actually see something. Then she shrugged at the screen, "Everything's fine?"

Barbara vowed that when she made her next call, she would time it for when Calvin was supposed to be up there. She was not just wasting time here she was wasting money in her budget that she could ill afford. She signed off and got up out of the chair. As Barbara was walking for the back door a certain object instantly registered in her brain. She stopped, reached down on the console and picked up the phone with the pink cover and little flower stickers all over the back.

Barbara held the phone up for the boy to see and then asked him, "Did you see who left this here?"

The boy stopped sweeping and just shrugged, "What is it?"

Barbara damn well knew what it was. The boy probably did too but no matter what useful information he might know, it was obvious to Barbara that he was going to keep it to himself. That made Barbara more than a little antsy. There was also very little she could do about it and in the back recesses of her mind she wondered if she even should. For the moment, Barbara simply pocketed the phone and left the building. She walked over to the admin building where she had to sign one form after another so these people could get paid and she could get her avgas. There were also the usual field fees and other assorted charges that came with an operation like this. What was not a normal thing was what Barbara saw across the tarmac.

Why was it that Barbara had a sneaking suspicion that the guys and the bird parked on the other side of the field, were not going to be paying anything to use this place? The aircraft was of a type that Barbara had seen parked out at Riggins Field back home. It had huge wings with imbedded turbo fans. It was painted in a grayish blue camouflage scheme and had a small cockpit and fat belly that looked less than aerodynamic. It also had an iron cross painted on the tailfin and probably in a few other places that Barbara could not see.

Lucy Rayne came walking out of the admin building when she noticed that Barbara had not come in. Lucy could guess why. She stopped next to Barbara and joined her in looking across the field, "Yeah they came in last night while you guys was sleeping."

Barbara was a little bit concerned so she asked, "Is this normal, Lucy?"

Lucy just shrugged, "Well we can't stop 'em if they do. They've been here before but normally they just kind of ignore us up here at Valley. Only good thing I can say is at least they don't use none of our gas cause they sure as hell don't pay for nothing else they take. What do those things run off of anyway? Never heard tell of nothing like that."

What could Barbara say to that? She knew it was a military vehicle and they had their own power sources that worked kind of like batteries. Barbara knew those power plants eventually wore out and had to be replaced. She watched the Germans take one out down at Riggins one day after they first arrived. It literally looked like a giant panel with a few pipes running around it and it slid right out on a standard forklift. Why they should make it so easy to replace was beyond Barbara since she had seen them change out more seats in those things than power plants. She had been told that a single cell could last for years and that most of the time the vehicle wore out long before its power.

Barbara had to ask, "They didn't say why they're here?"

Lucy just shrugged, "They never tell us anything. I don't even speak German."

When Barbara reached the bunkhouses, she found her daughter sitting at one of the outside tables eating from a plate of food that was piled unusually high. That was normal around these parts and it was considered impolite to not feed your guests to the point of their bellies exploding. It was so ingrained here that people made jokes about inviting armed robbers to dinner and then rolling them to jail afterwards. Barbara had come to suspect years ago that the custom was really just a disguise for the fact that everyone up here liked to eat their own body weight in food at every meal.

Barbara stopped at the table and laid her child's phone down in front of the plate she was eating from. With a smile that glossed over her stern tone, Barbara told Shannon, "We'll talk about this when we get home." After that,

Barbara went to the nearby cookhouse that seemed to run from before sunup till after sundown. She got her share with an overfilled plate that she was not so sure she could finish. As usual, they were burning a cow over a spit out back of the little shack, and they had a pot boiling next to the serving line that was full of the sticky substance they called grits. It was hot, steaming in the chilly morning air and it stuck to your ribs. Barbara thought it tasted kind of bland, but it did warm you up.

After chatting with a few people on the way back to the table, Barbara finally sat down and told Kent about the Germans. He seemed to think very little of it, but this did not really surprise Barbara. Kent never acted like anything was a big deal. She dropped the subject and then noticed with some alarm, "Where are they?"

Once again, Kent acted like nothing mattered at all, "Where are who?"

"Don't start, Kent," Barbara told him. "You know damn well who I mean." If anything, it was a bad sign that he picked just now to play ignorant.

"Mr. Tippet," Kent said with an optimistic tone, "was up early this morning sticking our tanks." He made eye contact with Barbara and added, "Which I might say was a very good idea. At any rate, one thing led to another and it would seem that Killian is having some problems with their fuel lines, so we will have to delay our departure for a little while longer."

Barbara sneered, "And that didn't answer the question."

"They went to town, Barbara," Kent relented. "It sounded harmless enough."

She pointed with her big thick spoon. It was the only kind that could handle the grits without breaking, "You were the one who warned me, remember?"

Shannon rolled her eyes at her mother, "Jesus Mom, Danni's always had the hots for Tony. How blind can you be?"

Now the spoon pointed in the teenager's direction and Barbara once again told her child, "We'll discuss how you know that later." She then shifted her attention back to Kent.

He jumped to his own defense before Barbara could get going, "And how was I supposed to stop them? I did mention that they might check with you first."

Shannon then jumped on her mother with, "Relax Mom. Tony just needed some stuff for the emergency kit. We had to dump a lot of that before we left. You know? To make room for Maxine? They're not going to be flying the hump at Sadley's Hardware."

"Shannon!" Barbara commanded with flared nostrils. She then made a command decision, "All right fine." She pointed her spoon back at Kent, "Only Danni stays with you today."

"I am fully aware," Kent replied, "that I suggested it Barbara. After sleeping on it, and knowing what we know now, I have changed my opinion on the matter."

"Danni can bitch about it all she wants," Barbara let it be known and her tone made it very clear that she did not care about anything else.

"It's not that," Kent told her. He took a printout from his jacket and put it on the table for Barbara to see, "I really do think we need to check out that transponder contact. We can't send Mr. Tippet up there alone and Miss Nguyen is hardly qualified to do my job so I can't go."

"Fine," Barbara mumbled as she began reading the paper. She continued in between reading words, "I'll do it and..."

"What?" Kent told her. "I certainly don't think that Mr. Tippet should be the one up at the station. You're the only one who knows where everything is. Not to mention, do you really want to drag Shannon out to the west slopes?"

Barbara was reaching the bottom of the page when she replied, "No, I was thinking about taking Danni with me. Shannon knows where everything is up at the station."

That inflamed Shannon, "You're putting this on me now?"

"Like it or not, Barbara," Kent remained calm enough, "Mr. Tippet is the best qualified to fly a search mission. He is most certainly the best candidate for this particular job. I talked with him this morning and after hearing the details, I'm not certain any other pilot would have even noticed that pinger."

Barbara thought about the paper she just read and then wondered what that had to do with what Kent just said. She was cautious, she was slightly paranoid, and she wanted to know, "Why is that exactly?"

"It was on a frequency that doesn't get used by bush pilots," Kent told her. "Even on its primary it was sporadic and weak. If anyone else had heard it they would have just written it off as a static burst, a solar flare, or something like that." In Barbara's mind that translated in to one thing. Tony was looking for an excuse to spend more time flying around and showing Danni all of the sights. Kent could see those thoughts in her eyes so he put it to her bluntly, "You can't go because we can't have both of our pilots in one vehicle and we need you at the station. I can't go because I'm needed here. That leaves you with the options of either Mr. Tippet flying alone out there..."

"Out of the question," Barbara injected since they both knew the answer to that. Flying around the island was one thing. There was plenty of communications, infrastructure, and if you had problems then you were never more than a few minutes from help. Out on the slopes it was an entirely different matter.

"There you have it," Kent told her. Then he mentioned, "Or you can let Mr. Tippet fly around with your daughter all day."

Barbara smiled and slapped her hand on the table, "Danni it is!"

CHAPTER 8

Tony was starting to wonder if just maybe he should have made a second attempt at horse borrowing. Years ago, not long after he had first joined the Rangers, on his very first visit to Valley Point he jumped the pasture fence and attempted to rope a horse for Idhitri because she wanted to ride one. Tony had a cousin who owned a couple of horses and he had ridden them enough so he figured how hard could it be? Unfortunately, most horses do not come to you like dogs even if Tony had seen some horses do that before. Maybe it was because these particular animals did not know him? No matter what the case, that little incident had put Tony's leg in a cast.

Now that he was sitting in the cab of this pickup truck listening to Danni and Killian sing away to some song on the guy's music list, Tony was starting to wonder if a broken leg might be less painful. He finally had to say something, "Killian, where do you find stuff like this? What is it?"

Danni developed a very 'Oh brother' kind of look and said to Killian, "Don't mind him, Kill. He's been a stick in the mud for weeks now."

"If you don't mind me saying," Killian stated in an easy-going manner. He even had a smile, but was still slightly cautious and delicately worded his reply, "I would have thought the situation might have been reversed. You know? Given your rather unfortunate incident, Daniella." As an afterthought he did mention, "You did get the flowers? Didn't you?"

Danni giggled and brushed his arm with her hand, "Yes I did and thank you very much, Killian. They were lovely." They both started laughing after she mentioned, "Lucy picked them out, didn't she?"

Tony was both cautious and curious when he asked, "You sent flowers?"

"Certainly," Killian replied in an upbeat way, "even if I had to defer to the better tastes of my sister. I would hope it is the thought that counts."

Tony became even more cautious,

"Where are you from again, Killian? You just got one of those weird accents. You like weird music. I was just wondering."

Danni pouted at Tony, "Do you mind? You know he is kind of our host and you did eat your share of that breakfast."

"Yeah," Tony shot back, "and we're paying for it too."

"It's all right," Killian blew the whole matter off and remained pleasant enough, "my father was from Beta Canaan. If you're wondering about my accent. New Celtland to be exact. He was working for Benthic, that is, if you were also curious about how he got here. He was a geologist."

That actually made Danni think about something else, "I wonder if that's where Kent's from?" Then she completely changed the subject and blindsided Tony with, "Which flowers did you send?"

To her surprise, Tony quickly came back with, "We took up a collection." It was not exactly the response that Danni had expected but she had not anticipated much of one at all. Then Tony changed the subject right back, "Lucy doesn't sound like you?"

"My sister," Killian told him, "was raised here."

Danni decided to play along, "So your mom really is from here? That's neat Kill, cause, you know, my parents were from different planets too. You don't really see too much of that."

Killian took his eyes off the road for a second and winked at her, "Indeed you don't. Maybe we should start a club?"

Tony huffed, "Oh you two have so much in common."

Danni developed an amusing look on her face, "Well we do like the same kind of music, you know."

That only caused Tony to slump in his seat, look out the window, and get huffy as he commented, "Sounds like somebody is pulling a cat through a meat grinder. What do you call this anyway?"

The description in no way diminished Killian's mood, "It's the traditional, classical, and ancestral music of my people. They're called the Rolling Stones."

The way that Tony was pouting was starting to make Danni feel a little bad. She eased off on the joyous attitude and noted, "You'll have to cut Tony some slack. He's been having some, well…"

"Do you mind," Tony became animated all over again, "not bringing my personal life in to this, Danni?"

Killian got the message loud and clear, "A certain redhead I take it. Just give her time, mate."

Tony went back to looking out the window and that made Danni feel like sliding down in the seat. She then took the first diversion that she could quickly find and pointed out the window at the little group of strangely dressed people that were walking down the road. Their clothing looked to be a few centuries out of date. Maybe even a few millennia? They were all dressed up in tasseled robes, thick belts, knee high boots, and that was not to even mention the strange hats with the excessive plumage. As they got closer, Danni got a better look at their shirts and pants. They were loose cut and covered in clasps and ties of the most impractical sort. As far as diversions went, this one was first class.

"Who the hell are those guys?"

It worked. Tony's mind had obviously changed gears and he was no longer slumped over on the window, "They're walking way out here? Where the hell are they going?"

Killian chuckled, "Probably to town."

Danni's head flipped as they passed the strangely dressed people who were starting to take on the shape of a little family. Now she got a good look at the woman's dress. It was puffy with a really low-cut neckline, complete with a corset that most definitely exaggerated her cleavage. Danni shivered at the very thought of wearing something like that. Then she saw Tony checking it out and said to him, "That's a really cute dress."

"How far out from town are we?" Tony asked.

"Oh, I don't know," Killian replied as even he took a good look in the rear-view mirror, "maybe two or three kilometers, give or take."

Tony whistled at that. It was not like he hadn't marched that far in the army plenty of times, only those weren't soldiers. The young looking adult woman was carrying a baby. They also had two or three toddlers tagging along as well. "Why don't we stop and give them a ride?"

"They wouldn't take it," Killian replied with confidence. "That right there, my friends, is some of the Father Jim Dove's indomitable flock."

Danni's head snapped back for another look. Her eyes were wide, "Those are Rennies?!"

Tony was trying to get a second look too. He sounded a bit confused, "I thought they all lived up in some big commune on the river."

"Common misconception," Killian replied. After making a right-hand turn, he added, "There is such a place. I've been there, took the tour actually. Most of them, though, have their own homes and are spread out all up and down Valley."

Danni settled back in her seat and found that she was still a bit stunned by their appearance, "Do they all dress like that?"

"In one fashion or another I suppose,"

Killian replied as if it were not that big of a deal.

Danni supposed that for him, it would not be. Despite the fact that the Rennies looked very out of place in these parts where the standard dress code usually consisted of long coats, Stetson hats, and blue jeans, he had to be used to seeing these people by now. Their numbers had been growing up here for several years. Danni was just not aware that any of them had migrated as far south as the river delta.

Since the strangely dressed people were long gone the last word said about them was by Tony who simply commented, "Kent's going to have his hands full." No one disagreed.

Danni found that she had largely forgotten about the incident when they reached the outskirts of the Valley Point settlement. Everything here looked normal enough to her eyes or at least it looked normal enough for Valley Point. It was not exactly a small town and was probably the largest one on the continent. It was still tiny compared to the bigger cities out in the Arch. Yet it came close enough to civilization if you just ignored all of the cowboys.

They parked right in front of the

hardware store and Danni could never get over her amazement at how Killian never failed to get a parking space right at the place he wanted to be. There was nowhere back home that you could ever do that. Despite the rustic nature of life on the continent, it did have some advantages. Danni decided to stand around on the sidewalk and take in some of those. Tony protested and seemed disgruntled when Danni blew him off. After he walked in the hardware store, she rolled her eyes and sighed.

Killian put his cowboy boot up on a short concrete hitching post and leaned over on his knee. He tilted his cowboy hat back and licked his lips as he looked up at Danni with a very serious and questioning glare. It made Danni a bit self-conscious and she snapped at him, "What?"

"I don't mean to pry, Daniella," he said diplomatically.

She crossed her arms and feet, "But you are anyway."

"Well," Killian remained light in tone, "since you chose to involve me, I do feel as if I might should ask."

"What?" Danni began to twitch, "What

are you talking about, Killian?"

He threw his arms up in the air and acted as if he had given up. Then he walked up on the front porch of the store and squared off with the girl as he told her, "I think the only person in the truck who did not notice what you were doing, was the one person you were hoping would."

Danni found it hard to look him in the eye, "I don't know what you're talking about."

"All right, love," Killian told her. "Have it your way." He then reached out and Danni flinched at his approaching hand. His fingers stopped as quickly as they had started. She was still somewhat defensive as he then thumped the breast pocket of her jacket. The contents shook like the sound of beads and Killian noted, "Those won't help, my dear."

How did he know? That struck a chord of fear in Danni, but her response was one of belligerence, "Who told you?"

"Your secret is safe with me, Danni," Killian remained light, "I suppose that you just under-estimate my powers of observation, is all."

81

Danni began to fidget even more as she meekly asked, "What do you want?"

Killian put his hands back like she was radioactive, "Nothing. I just want to make sure you are all right. After all love, you had two bullets pass through your body since we last parted company."

"Um," Danni still fidgeted. She was starting to wonder if she had done too good of a job back in the truck. Damn it! Why can't anything go as planned! She finally figured all she could say was, "Thanks?"

"Don't mention it," Killian began to walk away. When he was back down on the street he turned and said, "It would just be preferable that if you ever feel such a need as to require my services in the future, it might be a good idea to inform me first."

This guy was such a strange man. Danni also could not help but find him charming too. Damn, whatever he was doing, it sure worked better than anything she could come up with. A smile cracked on her lips and she had to ask him, "Oh yeah? Well, what would you do then?"

He thought about it for a second and then

replied, "In this particular instance, I think that I might inform you that subtle will never work here." He practically bowed and then said, "Now if you will excuse me, my dear. I have to check my office while I'm in town."

CHAPTER 9

It was the last thing that Leslie had expected. Then things went from strange to just plain bizarre. She did it anyway and for a quick moment she even questioned the sanity of working for the CG. If things were going to be like this all of the time, then she could see a resignation in her future. There were certainly a lot of jobs out there that paid a hell of a lot better than this one. It was just a sad truth that whoever said, crime does not pay, was just a sad and pathetic sap that was incompetent at whatever he was doing. Still, Leslie figured she would give them a little more time. It could be fun after all.

She parked her car under some trees of First Landing City Park. The person she was supposed to meet was pretty easy to spot. It was not that he was leaning up against the front fender of his car, there were others doing that.

It was more in how he was dressed and for the short time that Leslie had known the man, she had never seen him dress all that differently than he was now. She skipped up to him and with a huge grin she asked, "Gee I didn't know you trusted me this much, Norm. I thought I was like on probation or something."

Where Leslie was being quite cheerful, Norm was his usual angry self, "Yeah well that's Barbara's bullshit. I know you can handle yourself."

"Nice to know," Leslie was beaming. "So, you really do trust me now?"

"Hell no!" Norm told her. So far up till now, Norm had had not paid her much attention at all. Of course, the current round of attention was fleeting, and Leslie noted that the guy was more fixated on something way over on the other side of the park. He had a pair of binoculars and would take the occasional peak. When he finally did make eye contact with Leslie, he told her, "But you can handle this. Think of it as a test."

Leslie acted a little more seriously, "Ohhh-Kay, what do I have to do?"

He handed her the binoculars and then

pointed down the hill towards the running track. He then told her, "See if you can make out anything significant out there."

It took her all of five seconds to spot what he had to be talking about and then say, "That's Barton out there, isn't it?"

"Yeah," Norm replied as he made himself more comfortable and then crossed his arms. His basic sneer remained, "Tell me. When you're running a surveillance, what is the one big thing you look for?"

Still with the glasses over her eyes, Leslie told him, "That's easy. You look for any change in patterns and routines."

Norm waved his hand towards the running track, "See anything unusual about this set-up?"

Leslie actually looked away from the lenses for a second and thought about it. Then she answered, "Yeah, he normally runs the driveway every morning. He came to a park and he's running on a track now?" She went back to looking.

"Exactly," Norm said as if he were not really all that impressed. Personally, he was not sure that he was but at least this girl gave better answers than he would have probably expected from anybody else.

"So," Leslie said as she kept watching Jake jog around the distant track, "He does know we're here doing this, right? I mean, is this the test?"

All Norm said was, "Whatever you want to call it." Norm looked over his shoulder and back down towards the other end of the parking area. The stations four-by-four was still sitting where Jake had left it about a half hour ago. When he finished running, he would probably come back up this way and pick it up. What Norm was wondering was could Jake notice Leslie? The girl was pretty good at blending in. Norm knew that he would get spotted in a hot minute.

Leslie, still watching with the binoculars, became excited and sounded like she was a cheerleader as she told Norm, "Think I just spotted another change in routine."

Norm got off his butt and tried looking without the aid of anything. It was a good distance, so he had to ask, "What happened?"

"Um," Leslie said, "would you call

hopping the fence on the far side of the track, then jumping in a waiting car, a change in routine?"

Norm exploded, "Damn it! Is there any sign he made us?"

Leslie handed back the binoculars since there did not seem to be any reason to use them anymore, "I don't know, unless you count the middle finger he pointed at me when he rode off."

A few choice words escaped Norm's lips as he stomped around. When he calmed down, he began to rub his chin and think this through. He then realized he did have one card to play. He had an extra key to the station's car. Jake was going to have to come back for it. Wouldn't he? Norm looked back to the white four-by-four and then he blinked, rubbed his eyes, and took another good look. It was gone! How did he get back over here so fast and get it? That was impossible! It was time for another round of choice words.

Leslie was far less emotional about it, "Did I pass?"

Norm had to settle down before he could think about it some more. He quickly asked,

"You did get the make of the car, right?"

Leslie was practically glowing as she turned her nose up at Norm, "That's a rookie question, Norm."

"Did you!?"

"Of course, I did," she told him. Then, when he was getting antsy, she told him, "Course it doesn't really matter because I got something even better." Leslie knew when she had someone on the hook, and she loved the reeling in part better than all the rest. That was the fun after all, "Had a sticker on the door. It belonged to A.N.T. news."

Norm's eyes bulged. Then he realized the significance and suddenly felt like he now had one up on Jake. If nothing else, he had gathered his first bit of useful intelligence today. The only problem with that was what he mumbled to himself, "Jake, you stupid muther…"

Leslie interrupted him and was quite giddy, "This is kind of fun, Norm. What's next?"

"Next for you is back to the station," Norm told her.

Leslie wanted to pout but what little of it she did was only for show and she knew it. Norm was clearly the stubborn type. So much for the non-boring day. When she finally walked into the commissary at the station, she began reevaluating her dread of the situation that involved a moody redhead that kept dreaming up new sequences of buttons to push for no apparent reason.

Cal was busy at his desk. Leslie was starting to wonder if the guy ever got up from there. This time was a little different though. Everybody at the station was gathered around and watching his computer screen with great interest. Even the dog had finally gotten up off his pillow and was trying to nudge his way into the little circle.

It was Garcia that looked up first and saw Leslie standing there holding the screen door open, "Get in here and close that door, girl. You letting them vermin in."

As Leslie complied it was Bob Johnson who spoke next, "Where have you been?"

"Errands," Leslie told them as she walked up and peeked over Garcia's shoulder. She then noted, "I didn't think the Longhorns were playing Valley until next week."

"Naaa," Garcia told her, "this game is better."

Leslie noticed that Amy was kind of holding back and looking nervous. For that reason, Leslie figured that the redhead would be the best one to ask or in this case Leslie just pointed to the computer screen and gave the girl a 'What gives?' look. Amy seemed agitated but she did answer, "Norm called us. He wanted us to look over the feeds on the Alpha News Tap."

So that's what his game was. Leslie took another peek at the screen and noticed they were concentrating on the stories by one specific reporter. Leslie wondered if this Jessica Walsh was the driver of the getaway car. Then Leslie noticed that she was being intently watched, more than the video screen even, by Amy. It was not that big of a deal since the girl had been doing it ever since they started sharing the comwatch. This time, Leslie could not help but suspect, it was a little different.

Leslie decided to head off Amy by asking, "Why can't he just do this on his own phone?"

That seemed to divert Amy's attention for some reason. Leslie had only meant it to head off the question, but she would take a diversion which was even better. Amy said nothing and that included answering the question. It was Cal who did that, "Cause it's Norm we're talking about. He barely knows how to answer his phone."

Bob wanted to laugh at that, "He sure knows how to make calls when he's got a hair up his ass."

Garcia acted offended, "Come on, Bob. This is Norm we're talking about so give the man his due. That can't be true." Then Garcia finished his thought by saying, "Cause Norm's always got a hair up his ass."

"Point," Bob replied.

"Whoa," Calvin said as he reached for his headset and slipped it on. He silenced everybody in the room as he began placing a call with his computer screen. He then let out, "Think I found what he's looking for here."

Bob was a bit surprised, "Isn't that our car?"

Amy seemed very monotone today, "that's the one Jake usually drives." After she said it, Amy did give Leslie a look that could be interpreted as 'nasty', but Leslie chose not to take it that way. She simply shrugged and said, "I have no idea, gang. I just work here."

On the screen, the reporter was standing in a parking lot with quite a bit of activity going on. As Cal pulled up an icon to place his call, he hesitated for a second and thought that the activity he was seeing was kind of familiar. Then he saw a girl in a short pink skirt, carrying a big tray, pass behind the reporter. What was even more interesting was that this girl was on roller skates.

Cal held off dialing and just asked, "Is that where I think it is?"

Jessica Walsh spoke into the camera and confirmed Calvin's suspicions. She gestured to the stations four-by-four and said, "and as you can see behind me, even Colonial Government agencies have gotten in on the act. Your government wants you to know that the streets are safe. As you can see, this Foo King Restaurant, sight of the recent car bombing, is open for business and judging by all the cars, I'd say it's just Foo King great. For A.N.T. This is Jessica Walsh reporting."

Leslie's face distorted to the point of looking painful. She then asked, "She really gets paid to say stupid shit like that? I'm in the wrong line of work."

Everyone's attention turned to Cal as he yanked the headset off and held it a good distance from his head. He had obviously gotten Norman on the phone since they could hear the miniaturized sound of crackling profanity coming out of the speaker. When it slowed, Calvin finally put the headset back on and after a very short conversation, one in which he could barely get a word out, Cal thumped the icon and closed out the call.

Then he said to everybody, "Gar, you and Amy get the extra keys and go get our car. It's at that…"

"Yeah I know," Garcia said. "It's the one up at the end of the L-5. One question though. What's Jake going to do for a ride? For that matter, what do we tell him when we pick it up?"

Amy raised a finger and meekly asked, "Has something happened to Jake?"

"Guys," Cal told them with his own frustration plainly evident, "you know as much as I do right now. Just go get the car, ok?"

As they turned out of the driveway and onto the hard top, Garcia looked over from behind the steering wheel and asked the very silent Amy, "So what's up your ass today?"

Amy did not appear to take that question so well, "Could you have been any more crude, Garcia?"

"Yeah," he shot right back, "but that don't answer the question."

Amy's eyes widened and then suddenly she grabbed the huge bag that served as her purse. Garcia often thought that she had stolen it off some bag lady from downtown. Amy furiously pushed her way through an assortment of junk and then she slapped her forehead and with great frustration she kept going, "Shit! Shit! Shit!"

"What?" Garcia was a bit concerned.

Amy exploded, "I didn't know I was going out today! My badge, my ID cards, my whole wallet is sitting on my nightstand!"

"Oh Jesus," Garcia replied. "Every time, Amy. Why is it there's always something going on with you?"

Amy was on the verge of a meltdown now, "Never mind, Garcia. We're just going to pick up a car. It's not that big of a deal."

After they drove for another ten minutes, Amy noticed they were making the wrong turn. She pointed right when Garcia was turning left. Then Amy asked, "The L-5 is that way. Where are we going?"

"Your place," Garcia told her. "If you going to be out here with me, you're going to have what you're supposed to. It's not far out of our way."

Amy winced, "You sure?"

"I'm doing it ain't I?" He then went on by definitively stating, "And Amy, make sure you got your gun too, ok?"

CHAPTER 10

It was really not that different than an app you would download on your phone except that this one was specifically for the display screen on the chopper's instrument panel. Lucy had uploaded it for them before they flew out of Valley Point and back to the western slopes. When Danni had first turned it on, she thought the screen looked like one of those meters that some music players had, the kind that would jump to the beat of a song. Lucy had explained, "That's pretty much what it is, sugar. Only this one dances to the kind of bands you don't hear on your car radio."

When Tony and Lucy tested the meter, Danni was a little confused, "I don't get it. Why can't we just put it on my phone?"

As Lucy had been packing up her test gear, she pointed upwards to just above the chopper's bubble at a pair stubby looking bullhorn shaped items that Danni had never even really noticed before. Lucy explained, "Those are your chopper's wireless antennas. That's not something your phone has on it. Down in the cockpit, the instruments and com systems only use part of the frequencies that the antenna can pick up. This meter just lets you know when you're getting another part of the spectrum."

Danni thought about it and asked, "You mean like an emergency beacon? Only I thought they transmitted on regular frequencies?"

Lucy shrugged to that question and then replied, "Some of them do." What was that supposed to mean?

As they flew out to the slopes, Danni spent a good deal of her time reading the instructions for this very bland looking application. Other than the meter it had some slides that allowed you to tweak things like the sensitivity and the gain. She had no idea what any of that meant and came to realize that she needed a second set of instructions to explain the first. She was also scared to just start arbitrarily fiddling with the slides and options. Danni thought that if she did then she might accidentally bring the chopper down or something like that.

Tony actually laughed at that idea. He did point out however that they were being charged for the application. He also managed to use Killian's name instead of the airport's. Danni was really regretting her plan now. Finally, she tried to get him off the subject of Killian by asking, "What about Amy?"

The answer that Tony gave was pretty easy to predict, "What about her?"

Danni felt like she had screwed up all over again. She had practically heard his answer in her mind before he had ever said it, even before she asked her question! You would think that under such circumstances she would have been ready for it. Danni was not and she just kept her mouth shut after that. At least it got Tony distracted from Killian, which made Danni feel guilty. Before yesterday he had never thought twice about the guy.

For the next hour, the meter remained silent and so did Tony. Then out of the blue he said over the intercom, "I think there's somebody else."

Danni's eyes opened wide, "What? What are you talking about?"

"With Amy," Tony said with some measure of frustration. "You asked me what about her. I'm telling you."

Danni became confused and told him, "Tony, I asked you that over an hour ago..." After she thought about it, "And I'm not sure that's exactly what I meant anyway."

She noticed that he was not really looking in her direction. Sure, he had to watch where he was going but there was just not that much risk of hitting a tree when you were flying between five and ten thousand feet in the air.

Tony was not looking at her even with his sunglasses on.

Then he asked the unexpected, "Was that really an hour ago? Time flies when you do, I guess."

That actually brought about a giggle from Danni, even if she was not sure that he had meant for it to. At least Tony did not seem to take offense. Danni recovered her wits and apologized. Tony let her off the hook even if her amusement had obviously rankled some feathers. It was one of those things that Danni really liked about him. He might not act it, but Tony always had a way of putting others before himself.

Finally, Danni said, "I'm sorry, Tony. I guess I really can't understand what you're going through."

"Sure you do," he waved that notion off in a hurry. "You're really pretty, Danni. I'm sure you've had some girlfriends before."

Tony had managed to climb the mountain and fall off the cliff in the space of less than two seconds. Danni exploded on the intercom, "I'm NOT GAY!"

Tony actually had to pull his headset off and clean out his ears with a finger. When he put them back on, he then did something that he had not managed since they left the Arch. He looked at her while he was flying, raised his sunglasses, and seriously asked, "You're serious?" Danni did not dignify that with a response. She simply crossed her arms and looked at the display screen on the instrument panel. The little meter was still dead. All the while Tony was stumbling over an apology, although judging by his tone it was clear that he was not even really sure he believed her.

Awkward silence returned and it was Danni who finally blurted out, "Leslie's gay."

Tony did not even hesitate in responding, "No, she's not."

There was fire in Danni's eyes as her head snapped towards Tony and she accusingly asked him, "How do you know?"

If Tony acted worried about it then he did not show it. If anything, he sounded confused when he replied, "How else? She told me. I mean not in so many words, but she talks about guys like she's drooling on something."

Danni backed off. She proceeded with

caution, "You mean? You? Her? You two? Haven't? You know?"

"What's with all these questions?" Tony was even more confused now. He actually started considering things and Danni got nervous all over again. Finally, he just said, "Leslie's kind of like the brother I never had, if that makes any sense."

Danni was dumbstruck by that. She replied with a gaping tone, "Tony, um, you have six or seven brothers. I think. I lost count."

"I know," Tony replied, "and she's like the brother I wished I had." After playing with his words he said, "You don't get it, Danni. You were an only child. I was the youngest of a pretty large family. You might have noticed that all my brothers and cousins are firemen and I'm not." Tony even had to qualify that much, "Except for the one petty crook, two used car salesmen, an electrician, a jewelry store salesman and we must not forget Kevin who is still living in Aunt Jean's basement. Course, he did place third in that Music Hero game competition so maybe we're letting him back in to the reunion next year."

Danni knew exactly what she wanted to ask him now but there was no way in hell she could make herself do it. Instead she asked, "So what was your problem with Killian this morning? You don't think, I mean, you know? Him and Amy?"

Tony quickly waved the notion off, "Oh hell no. I mean I know better than that."

"Then what was it, Tony?" Danni pushed him to the point of almost demanding. Naturally she framed the question to leave her a way out, "You know we do have to get along with the Raynes. They help us out up here, a lot. Not to mention, Killian is a nice guy."

If Tony were not flying, Danni suspected he might have flown off the handle right about now. His actions remained calm even if his voice had something of an edge, "Of course he is. That's the problem."

Danni shrugged, "I don't get it?"

"Danni," Tony sounded serious and almost pleading, "the guy is everything I'm not. He knows how to control himself. He's handsome, he's kind of dashing, he knows what to say and when. He knows how to keep his mouth shut. I don't ever do any of those things. I wish I could, but I just can't even make myself do it."

Danni reached out and touched his arm. Tony didn't seem to notice. He had on a thick jacket and no matter why he did not, that's what it looked like to Danni. She still went, "You're a great guy, Tony. I wouldn't worry about that."

"Thanks, Danni," he replied to her. "I appreciate the sympathy, I really do. It's just, it's not going to help right now."

At least there was work! Danni let out a heavy sigh and let her eyes fixate on the little monitor in front of her. It was proving to be just as dead as everything else at the moment. She realized she was pretty snitty when she asked Tony, "You sure this is the area?"

Tony did not notice her tone, "The waterfalls are about two klicks south of our position, we're dead on."

"Well there's nothing on this little app," Danni told him. "Want me to play with it a little? Maybe we'll get lucky?"

If Tony had any perceptions about the nature of Danni's last sentence, he sure kept it to himself. He didn't even make it into a joke. He just sounded straight and flat as he said,

"Can't hurt."

There was nothing left for Danni to do besides what she said she would, literally. She reached out on the little screen and tapped into the program's options menu. It gave her a new set of slides and each one had a name that she had never seen before. Danni bit her bottom lip as she thought about it and then finally, she just shrugged and said, "Oh well." She slid the little bars to the left and the right. Nothing happened. Then she tried a new configuration and yet again, nothing happened. Then, Danny saw the button at the bottom of the screen. It said 'apply' so she tapped it with her current configuration.

The chopper went bang!

Danni jumped back in her seat and in a terrified voice she screamed, "I didn't do that! Honest to god! Please tell me I didn't do that!"

At least Tony did not seem particularly worried. He was busy looking down at the ground, but it was not in a panicked kind of way. He even had time to tell her, "You didn't do it, relax."

There was no relaxing when your helicopter went bang. Danni even saw some black smoke swirling away from them. It wasn't much and it quickly dispersed but that still could not be good. All of it made Danni think of a million questions but she decided they could all be summed up into just one, "Are we gonna die?"

"Hell no," Tony replied in a very calm voice. He was flying lower to the ground! Then he actually explained in an even voice, "You saw me sticking the tanks this morning?"

"Um," Danni's eyes got bigger as they got closer to the ground. "Yeah? I thought you were just seeing how much gas we had."

"I got fuel gages for that, Danni," he was a bit distracted now. "I was checking the fuel quality." There was no reply since, to Danni at least, they were moving kind of fast to be this low. For Tony, who was obviously concentrating, he seemed to be talking as much for his own benefit as hers, "We took a long trip. That meant we burned off more fuel than we usually do. Guess what happens inside a fuel tank in a humid climate like we live in?"

"Uh," Danni was pushing back on the seat rather hard. The seat was winning the fight as she asked, "You crash and die?"

"Condensation," Tony told her.

"Then you crash and die?"

Tony reached over and tugged at her safety harness. He seemed to be satisfied but Danni reached down and pulled it even tighter. As the ground got really close, Danni closed her eyes and began to scream. She got louder when it felt like her body had just slammed into a wall.

CHAPTER 11

"What are we doing?" Amy protested once again. She pointed out across the parking lot at the station's empty vehicle that was parked at the edge of the Foo King parking area and then told Garcia, "There it is, right there!"

Garcia was mostly ignoring her. He was busy looking around the parking lot and subsequently waiting on his order to arrive. He kept his sunglasses on even if there was not much of a need for them today. The sky was kind of cloudy which was not unusual for the past few weeks. There were quite a few things that were, however. That's why Garcia decided to take advantage of the situation and really talk to Amy. He didn't bother explaining himself though, "You and Tony are getting on everybody's nerves, you know that, right?"

Amy snorted, "That's nobody's business but ours."

"I beg to differ, girl," Garcia replied. "You two done gone and made it everybody's business. What's worse, you done gone and made it Barbara's business. What's the number one rule of the Ranger Code these days?"

It was clear to Amy that he was not talking about the official manual, which she was not even sure anyone had ever read. No, Amy was sure that he was talking about Garcia Alvarez's Ranger Code. She cited rule number one, "Don't wake the dragon?"

"Exactly," Garcia told her with a pleased sounding voice. Then he got a little bit frustrated, "And you two numb nuts went and had that little snit in the commissary yesterday morning."

Amy was quite adamant when she protested, "I didn't do that. That was Tony." After Amy had a few moments to think about it she wondered and asked, "Is this why Calvin sent me instead of Bob? He wanted you to have a talk with me?"

Garcia almost laughed, "Girl, I ain't got a clue why he sent you. In fact, I ain't got a clue about a lot of things lately. That's why we're just sitting here right now."

Amy rolled her eyes, "Killing time so we don't have to deal with all the crap at the station or just because you think the waitress is cute?"

"Both actually," Garcia replied. Then he also said something smart, well sort of smart, "And I want to see what's going on before we make a move."

"Make a move?" Amy did not sound convinced, "Garcia, we're just here to pick up a car."

"You so sure about that?" Garcia took another quick scan of the parking lot, "How many times we ever done this before?" Amy thought about it, but Garcia beat her to the punch, "How about never? You don't think that sounds a little funny?"

"God," Amy sighed in disbelief, "and I

thought Bob was the paranoid twin."

"Hey," Garcia protested, "the guy has an insurance company trying to steal his car. I think he earned a few paranoid points." When Amy had nothing to say about that, Garcia lowered his glasses just a little and scanned the parking lot again. His eyes stopped at the window where the orders were picked-up by the skating waitresses. His waitress was there and the tray that she was loading down looked right. So did her legs for that matter.

Amy somehow noticed and told him, "Would you stop that already? You know, I am sitting right here."

Garcia's eyes swung to her and looked at her over the top of his shades, "And you are trouble with a capital T."

"That is not what I mean, Gar," Amy protested. "There is such a thing as just being polite, you know?"

Garcia laughed and went right back to watching the waitress, "So, the truth comes out. You still like him, don't you?" She tried but Garcia cut her off, "And don't even play that 'who' crap with me. You know damn well who I mean." Amy just pouted in response. Gar wanted to laugh again, "Thought so. What I don't see is what the problem is. You two were cruising along just fine for almost two years. Hell, even Bob's wife kept rattling on about how she was going to decorate your wedding cake and shit."

Amy's eyes widened and her head snapped to attention, "She didn't? I mean, she wasn't? You're kidding right?"

"Hell no," Garcia told her bluntly. "Course I think that woman eats more cakes than she decorates but she definitely got them on the brain almost twenty-four seven. Every time Bob brought you two up, she was practically glowing." Garcia also mumbled, "And salivating."

Amy slid down in the seat and began to squirm, "Oh god, I am so embarrassed."

Now Gar got animated, "You see, girl, that's what I'm not getting about all this shit. What was it? What did he do, I mean besides being Tony? You should have already been used to that."

"God, Gar!" Amy grunted. "Can't a girl just change her mind without everybody having a fit over it?"

"Sure she can," Garcia told her, "except when she don't. I'm not so convinced you have. Which brings me right back to the point. What happened? Don't tell me it was that Leslie chick either, cause this all started before she came around."

Amy went right back to pouting, "It's complicated." Before Garcia could contradict that statement, Amy went on the offensive, "Tony put you up to this, didn't he?"

Garcia snorted a laugh, "Hell no. You did." Amy was too shocked to say anything, so Garcia told her flat, "When you two started making the rest of our lives complicated." She was about to deny it. What else could she say? Garcia would not let her get that far. He quickly pointed out, "And I'm not just talking about your little row the other morning. How about leaving your badge and shit at your place? How about blowing off the new girl instead of showing her how to run coms? How about..."

Amy put her hand up, "Ok, Gar, point made already!"

"Amy," Garcia replied, "I don't want you to just get a point. I want you to pull your head out of your..." The waitress set her tray down on the vehicle's open window and Gar went right to a smile as he changed his sentence, "As I was saying. That looks really delicious." He handed his card over to the girl and asked, "Now you know my name. What's yours?"

The waitress in pink took his card and giggled, "Betsy! Nice to meet you," she looked down at his plastic and went on, "Garcia. Sure your wife doesn't want anything?"

Amy sneered, "Not even close."

Garcia quickly replied, "That's my coworker."

That seemed to perk Betsy right up before she ran off with the payment. That left Garcia giggling like he was the schoolgirl. Amy on the other hand was less than impressed. She rolled her eyes and slapped her forehead, "Please tell me my gender is not that stupid." She then grunted at Garcia, "That's your line? Now you know my name...."

Garcia seemed proud of himself, "It worked didn't it?"

Amy was done with this. She went to open the door and told Gar, "I'm just going to drive back to the station, ok?" She stopped when she realized something, so she held out her hand, "Keys?"

"Just wait a minute, girl," Garcia was certain he had the entire situation in hand. Amy had very little choice in the matter, so she sat there with her arms crossed, pouting. Betsy the waitress came rolling back on her skates and Garcia spent a few minutes making her laugh and flirting. It was enough to make Amy want to puke. Finally, he did do something relevant, "You didn't see who drove up in that car over there, did you? You know, the one like we're in?"

At first, Betsy was completely confused. Then it was like somebody turned on a light bulb and she enthusiastically said, "Oh my god. Your cars do look alike. Did you buy it at the same lot or something?"

Garcia noticed the strange look on Amy's face. The girl's eyes had gotten big and her jaw was wide open. She made eye contact and had the most serious, 'You have got to be kidding me' kind of faces. Garcia just shrugged and happily got back to the flirting. He slapped the logo on the side of his vehicle and said, "Not exactly, you know what this is?"

Betsy looked down at the colonial seal on the door and then pointed to the other vehicle, "It's the same as that one?"

"Hell yeah," he told her. "I sell these." That made Betsy excited.

It made Amy annoyed, "Give me the fucking keys, Gar."

Garcia did as ask, and they both slipped out of the car. Betsy's arms went right for Garcia's. She looked like she was trying to steady herself on the roller skates. Garcia looked down at her feet and then he asked her, "You must be new."

"Oh," Betsy told him, "very. Thanks for helping me stay up."

"No problem," Garcia told her. He then started pulling her along, across the lot. Every now and then they would hit a crack or bump and Betsy would almost fall over. Gar always came to the rescue. Then they reached the other vehicle and Amy was having a time with the door. On the other hand, Garcia was having a very good time, so he was quite upbeat when he asked Amy, "What's up, girl?"

Amy was very frustrated, "The key won't

fit!"

"What?" Garcia left Betsy and walked over to relieve Amy of the keys. Unfortunately, his bravado was not enough to get the door opened ether. He grumbled for a moment, "Damn, Cal, he gave us the wrong keys."

Amy shook her head in resignation, grabbed Garcia's hand and held it up so that he could see the tag on the key chain that he was holding, "I'm not that stupid, Gar. Look at the bumper number. This is the right set."

Garcia really did not get it. What he did get was the twisted coat hanger that was laying right on the hood of the car. He slapped the keys back in Amy's hand and grabbed for the coat hanger. He proudly proclaimed, "I'll get this."

No sooner had Garcia forced the wire in the window, he heard a very commanding voice call out, "Step away from the car and keep your hands plainly in view!"

Amy tugged at Garcia's sleeve and pointed to the three police cars that had just driven up. She then meekly held up her hands and took a step away from the car. Garcia was a little more reluctant even though all six cops were standing with their hands on their weapons. They had not taken them out of the holster, but they were sure ready to do it. He tried to remain calm and told them in a friendly voice, "Whoa, relax guys. We're Colonial Officers, we just having key problems here."

The cop with the stripes was not that impressed, "Really? Well this vehicle was reported stolen a little while ago. If you're officers, then let's see some ID."

"Got my badge right here. I'm going to get it slowly," Garcia held his jacket out so they could see both his gun and his inner pocket. He reached with two fingers for the pocket. Then he became a bit embarrassed when he found the pocket empty, "I must have dropped it." Quickly and nervously Garcia told Amy, "Quick, girl, whip out your badge."

Amy still had her hands up and she was quite annoyed as she told him in a flat voice, "It's in my purse, Gar. You know, the one in the other car?"

Car! That was it! Garcia told the cops, "Yeah we drove over here in another vehicle just like this. Government logo and everything."

The cop looked around and then asked,

"What other car?"

Now Garcia looked around and suddenly became very alarmed, "Where the hell did our car go!"

Amy, still with her hands in the air, leaned forward and said, "More important. Where's the waitress?"

Garcia screamed, "That bitch jacked our ride!"

CHAPTER 12

"Not what you were expecting?"

Kent got down off the horse and was too busy looking around to even consider the question that Killian had asked. After hitching the horse, Kent wandered out into the middle of the muddy little path that served as the main street. He fully realized that there was probably more mixed in with the black soup than just wet dirt. There were plenty of animals running around here and the only form of transportation that was allowed was of the four-legged variety. The only good news there, was it would seem that most of the people could not afford such animals.

Kent did have an answer for the sheriff though, "Mr. Rayne, if you're asking me if I think this a poor attempt at recreating a medieval village then the answer is yes. If you were asking me if I was expecting a stonework castle, the answer is no." There was almost no stonework here of any kind. Most of the village was made of wood and that was about as close as this place came to being an authentic reproduction. The idea that the place was medieval was, to Kent at least, a sorry excuse for sloppy workmanship.

Dr. Dykstra got down off his horse and joined Kent in the road. Instead of looking around he pointed to the generally poor condition of the muddy street and said, "If there was ever a breeding ground for disease..."

Kent nodded, "Yes, Doctor, this is exactly the kind of situation that the Palace was concerned about. I shall convey to the Governor that you were not exaggerating in the least."

The mention of the Palace made Killian almost want to laugh, "I'm afraid that Crass is the least of our concerns out here." He nodded towards a couple of men that were standing around at the end of a row of semi-permanent looking tent structures. They were not dressed that differently than any of the others in the settlement. Kent thought it a poor attempt at dressing like one would suppose a medieval peasant might. There was one difference, however. Besides the fact that both men were unusually large, they also carried weapons.

"Swords?" Kent found it amusing and looked to Killian, "I don't suppose they think that such implements would deter the Wehrmacht?"

"I would hope not. Of course, the Germans do not seem to have much interest in what goes on here in Valley." Killian replied as he nodded towards a distant tower. It was nothing like you would see in a storybook fairy tale. It was crudely made with a skeletal support of logs, a platform that was semi barricaded and a thatch roof. Kent would have figured it was sufficient for being a lookout but nothing about it would stop bullets. The man who was currently pacing around on it was armed with a crossbow. Killian noted, "The Rennies have all kinds of rules and restrictions. Weapons are not among them."

Kent took it with a grain of salt and even

a bit of curiosity, "I would hope not, Mr. Rayne. There are still dangerous animals that lurk in these forests. I suppose edged weapons and archery would sufficiently handle most of them."

"Yes, that is true," Killian replied, "but not exactly what I was insinuating. The weapons they carry are also of sufficient volume and lethality to be more than a match for the weapons that the Governor has at her disposal. That being, none at all."

"I see your meaning," Kent replied and with a nod of appreciation he also noted, "I have to admit that had not occurred to me. Have these people given you any indication of hostile intent?"

"No," Killian admitted. "They are peaceful enough. They certainly don't bother the local farmers who tend to be armed with military grade firearms." He even went on further and admitted, "Usually when there is trouble I find it's the farmers or ranchers who started it."

"That being the case," Kent said, "let us handle one problem at a time, shall we?" Kent did quietly note to Killian, as they walked towards the three-story log structure, "I shall pass your concerns along to Chief Agent Reilly."

The overbuilt log cabin was not very lavishly decorated on the outside or in. It made Kent wonder about this man they were here to meet with. Jim Dove had the reputation back in the Arch of being a cult leader. Kent had never bothered to look into any of those rumors because up till recently there was no reason. People talked about the Rennies but to Kent at least it sounded more like the kind of thing that people did for amusement. The entire planet was on the whole a rather dull place. Anything out of the ordinary certainly rated conversation and the Rennies were most definitely that.

Kent did do some research when he found out he would be meeting with the man. The news reports on him were mostly useless. They were fluff at best. What little that Kent could find out came from a few reputable people who had made it their job to watch the most honored Father Dove. Kent was kind of surprised to find out that the man had not actually started the movement. There were some Rennies living out here before the war. Those original followers of this anti-technological movement had migrated to the colony from Henry's Star. They had apparently had any number of disagreements with the

Argentinean government that ran the largest colony there.

Jim Dove was a relative newcomer. The Rennies had already adopted pseudo medieval attire before he became a prominent figure in their religion. Now, he was most definitely their undisputed leader even if they lacked any official hierarchy. That much was very clear when he entered the room that he held his 'court' in. The man was surrounded by a group of heavily armed bodyguards, all of whom were wearing chain armor and carried two handed swords that they used for some little ceremony. They all had very fancy sir coats that looked to have been decorated by hand. Kent had no doubt that the design was supposed to be some kind of coat of arms.

The man himself was very much in contrast with that of his ceremonial guard. He was very plainly dressed in brown robes that lacked any decoration at all. He did not pull his hood off until after he sat on his 'throne.' It was carved and polished out of the stump of a huge tree that had obviously been left when they built this place around it.

If there was any other thing that Kent might have said to describe Dove, it was pleased. The guy was beaming, and he quickly clapped his hands and commanded a small army of servants, "Please, make our guests comfortable." Kent noticed the faces of his servants and they seemed rather eager to please this man. Kent did not see any fear or even a hint of dissatisfaction. What he was seeing from all of Dove's people was eagerness.

Jim Dove then went on by addressing his guests, "Welcome to the Barony. I am most certainly honored to meet with official ambassadors from the Office of Governor Crass." Dove got a little personal after that as he looked to Killian, "Sheriff, it's good to have you back. Doctor Dykstra, you look well." Then the man pointed out Kent, "And are you the Colonial Ranger?"

Kent nodded and introduced himself before asking, "And I would assume that I have the honor of addressing Mr. James Warren Dove."

It was the reaction that Kent was looking for. Dove did not seem to be all that distressed about how his name was used. He even made a joke out of it, "We're informal around here, Agent Gold. Why don't you call me Father Jim?"

It was not just Dove's reaction that Kent

noticed. There were several bodyguards, the 'knights' as Dove called them, who were standing behind the stump throne. A few of them did not seem to care for Kent nor how their leader was addressed. Kent would remember that.

"Now Gentleman," Dove stated as he clapped his hands again. Refreshments and tables were brought in along with plates of food and drink. He was certainly not holding back, and Kent got the idea that this little visit pleased him in the extreme. He told his guests, "If there is one thing we know how to do, that's eat."

CHAPTER 13

"It felt like a crash," Danni said as she sat in the open chopper door. She also pulled her jacket a little tighter and then shivered. She never thought she would miss the Arch this much. She certainly never missed sweating and humidity but right now she did.

Tony climbed down from the open engine cover and then picked up a rag that he proceeded to wipe his hands with. He also noted, "It was just a hard landing. I had some harder ones in the military when I was flying medivac. We still had power when we hit, you know?"

If that was a 'not so hard' landing, then Danni really did not want to experience a hard one. She gave a heavy sigh and then glumly stated, "Well we don't have power now." She looked at Tony and with a great deal of frustration and a little bit of fear, "Are we screwed? I mean is the... you can fix it right?"

Tony shrugged, "It's not that bad. Enough water must have gotten into the lines and past the filters. I was afraid of something like this... We got lucky."

"You call this lucky," Danni was horrified.

"Yeah," at least Tony seemed upbeat. "We could have been in the middle of the ocean on the way back home." Tony let that sink in and then he gestured to where they were, "We might not have found a field to set down in. If we'd come down in the trees, then we'd have lost the rotors and the bird. All kinds of other things could have gone wrong. That's what usually gets you killed when you're flying. One problem and you can handle it, usually. Get a

125

lot of things going against you and well you're..."

Danni held her hand up and nodded, "I get it already. So, what you're saying here is, you can fix this, right?"

"Sure," Tony tossed the rag aside and sounded upbeat. Then he was a bit more pissed when he continued, "If Chuck hadn't dumped most of the onboard took kit to make room for Maxine."

Danni jumped down out of the door and complained, "Why would he do that? I've seen that little space. You couldn't fit any of those crates in there."

Tony held his hands up for her to stop ranting and then he tried to calmly explain, "It's not his fault, ok? It wasn't a matter of space. It was a matter of weight. I knew about it and approved it."

Danni threw her arms in the air and twirled, "Oh fucking great, Tony. Fat lot of good it's going to do us with all our tools sitting back in Chuck's bunker buried in empty beer cans."

"It's not that..." Tony snorted, then he

laughed. Danni was not amused so he told her, "It's just that image is kind of well it's pretty dead on actually." Danni still had a sneer on her face when she squared off with him. Then, finally she broke down laughing too. Tony slapped her shoulder and tried to cheer her up, "Don't sweat it, kiddo. Barbara's got a full tool kit in her bird. We'll just call her and get her out here. I'm pretty sure she can land over there. I'll pull and clean the filters, and we should be back in the air in no time."

"Oh, don't worry," Danni told him, "I'm pretty sure that sweating is the one thing I will not be doing out here."

Tony even smiled now, "That's a good point. Ok, tell you what you go call Barbara and give her a sit rep. I'll go down the hill over there and see if I can scrounge up some firewood. That should keep us pretty comfortable until Barbara gets here."

Danni felt like smiling this time, "Thanks." She had a thought before she went to the chopper, "Um, why don't you go call Barbara and let me go get something to burn? After all, this is kind of your fault and I really don't want to get yelled at again."

Tony snickered and said, "Sure, do you

know what kind of wood you need to find?"

"Um," Danni thought about it and then meekly replied. The kind that grows on trees?"

"Exactly my point," Tony said as he started walking for the nearby tree line. He called back to her, "Trust me. I come from a long line of firemen."

Danni grunted before she yelled out at the departing Tony, "Yeah, well that means you'll be pretty handy putting it out! Till then!" If Tony had heard the last feeble protest, then he did not show it. Danni groaned and then walked back to the chopper. She slid in her seat and put the headset on. She punched the exit button on the application she had up and running.

The meter bar that she had been looking at most of the morning was still as dead as it had been since they tested it back at Valley Point. It was also not going away. Danni got frustrated with it and kept thumping the exit button harder and harder. When it proved it would not give up the screen, she tried to just minimize it. It still did nothing. Danni yelled at it.

The meter bar rolled across the screen like it was a wave. Danni blinked and jerked.

She even heard the static filled rumbling noise in the headset. Then it came again, and again. Danni's eyes got big, "Whoa!" She checked the signal strength and realized that whatever was pinging away out there was pretty damn close. Then it stopped just as quickly as it had started.

"Screw it," was all that Danni could think to mumble under her breath. She had bigger problems right now. She now knew that their first contact with the beacon was no phantom. That was good enough for the time being. Once the chopper was repaired then they would have plenty of time to look. Right now, she had to get Barbara on the radio and that was not going to happen as long as this stupid app was hogging the screen!

Nothing that Danni could do would make the app go away so, finally she did the only thing that you could do in such circumstances. She reached down behind the instrument panel and pulled the hardwire connection for the power source. The screen went blank and Danni sighed in relief, "'Bout damn time." She plugged the power cable back in and the screen came back to life. It began to boot up and she waited for it to finish. She waited some more. She waited even more. Finally, she got tired of waiting. The screen was hung up with the circle of spinning arrows of the restart cycle.

It was probably nothing. Danni figured that if Tony could pull fuel filters from a chopper engine, she was sure that he could get the computer to reboot. All that she had to do was just wait for him to get back. Danni decided to do that in the chopper since the one thing that it was really good at was deflecting the breeze. Despite that advantage, she could see her breath and to Danni who had grown up in the Arch that just seemed plain wrong. She was wearing two layers of clothing and a flight suit over that. How could she be cold?

The more uncomfortable she got the more Danni's eyes kept drifting down to the vest pocket that was just inside her flight suit. Finally, the waiting was a little too much. Danni shut her eyes and shook her head. She told herself quietly, "I deserve it this time." She really did not feel any pain at the moment but wasn't being cold a kind of pain? Danni pulled the zipper down just a little and reached in the pocket of her vest. She pulled out the little bottle, took out a pill, and then swallowed it without any water.

After a few minutes she felt a bit more eased. She laid her head back and tried to rest. The cold did not go away but Danni simply found she no longer cared or thought that much about it. She didn't really think much about anything at all for a little while until a stray thought ran through her mind. Where the hell was Tony?

Danni climbed down out of the chopper and looked around her immediate environs. Everything looked pretty much like it had when they had first landed. After walking around the chopper a few times, she finally realized that Tony was not there. Danni scanned the field as she began to feel panic welling up inside her. She began yelling for Tony after that and now she was definitely panicking.

A tear ran down her cheek and Danni discovered that she had lost her breath while screaming. She could barely speak when she grumbled, "Oh, shit."

CHAPTER 14

"Are you sure about that?"

The guy in the white beanie and the shirt that might have matched in color, had it not been stained in grease, gave Bob the evil eye as he answered, "That's what I told you, wasn't it?"

Bob had always wondered about this guy. He was big and burly, had a gruff voice and did he ever stand anywhere but this service window? It was like the window was a poster and this guy was the picture. He was such a permanent fixture that Bob often wondered why they didn't change this locations name from the Foo King Dinner to Mel's Dinner.

After the bombing, Bob was really surprised that they didn't just shut this place down but then again there was no Foo King like this anywhere else. All the other ones were just your typical drive thru and fast food eat in. Here, you could park your car under a little awning with menus at the window. The waitresses came right out to you. It was a different kind of Foo King that sort of made it special.

Bob figured he'd wasted enough time at this particular Foo King. He nodded to Mel and with a smile he told him, "Thank you, sir, you've been absolutely no help whatsoever."

Mel smiled and nodded back, "And I am so proud to have done my civic duty." He then went back to his normal scowl, "VERA! Get your ass out here! Your order is up!"

Bob walked back to his car and just stood by the door, surveying the parking area one last time. All he knew was that if Amy and Garcia had ever gotten here in the first place, then they were no longer. Neither of the station's vehicles were here either. What the hell had happened? Did Amy and Garcia pick up the other car? If they did, then why weren't they already back at the station? Why didn't they answer their phones?

Bob tried calling both Garcia and Amy one more time. There was still no answer, so he called the station and Leslie picked up. She had not heard from anybody either. He asked her, "What about Calvin?"

Leslie sounded insanely bored as she answered, "He hasn't either. Look, Johnson, have you ever thought about calling a cop?"

"What?" Bob was not particularly thrilled with the idea, "Call the city? Are you crazy? Those guys hate us, um, I mean when they even know who we are. Besides, us being law enforcement we can't just go make this some official…"

Leslie interrupted, "Who said anything about official, champ? Stay away from official.

Just talk to the guy who's working the zone. They usually know everything going on in their area. Course they usually don't do much about it but that can be helpful too."

Bob just blew it off, "They're not going to tell me squat, Leslie, you don't know those guys like we do."

"I beg to differ, big boy," Leslie shot back. "You just got to know how to ask."

"Wait a minute," Bob said as his eye caught sight of a familiar looking object that was slowly moving in front of the strip mall that the restaurant was located by. It was a white, four-wheel drive vehicle and it was definitely the right make and model. After a more careful look, Bob could see a round logo on the door as it parked right in front of this gym. Was that a colonial seal he was looking at? He told Leslie, "I think I found them. Let me call you back."

Bob could still hear Leslie saying something in protest as he hung up. He was not that worried either. He was about to get in his car when he stopped and took a second look at the white vehicle. Bob closed his door and figured he had better walk. The parking area for the diner and the mall were closed off from each other to keep people from cutting through to avoid the nearby traffic light. It took forever to change since it also handled the traffic for the L-5 on ramp.

As near as Bob could tell, there was still somebody sitting in that vehicle. If he tried to drive over there it would take forever and more important, he'd lose sight of it. Fortunately, it did look like the driver was on the phone. The guy even appeared to be looking his way. That was all good news because the closer he got the more certain he was that the logo on the side belonged to the CG. That had to be their vehicle. He even started picking out little details the closer he got, and by the time a random woman got his attention, he was positive that it was the car he was looking for.

The random woman actually tugged on his sleeve to make sure she got his attention. She had apparently just come out of the mall's grocery store and still had a half full cart of food and children. She pointed back towards the Foo King and asked, "Hey, mister, didn't I just see you walk away from that car?"

At first, Bob had no idea what she was talking about, but then he looked back to the Foo King. Another car had pulled up in front of his. A guy had gotten out of the passenger side and was now opening his car door so fast that the guy had to have a key! He proved it a second later as he cranked the vehicle up and then both vehicles drove away!

Bob went running in the direction of his vanishing car while screaming, "You sons of bitch's! Come back here!!!" He stopped running after only a few seconds. As he stomped back past the lady, she made a snide comment about car thieves and Bob grumbled back, "That was the insurance company!"

The woman got back to loading groceries in her car as she stated, "There's a difference?"

The only good news was that the station car was not only still parked in front of the gym, but the driver had gotten out and was going inside. Bob figured it had to be Garcia. He could not really tell from this distance but whoever it was kind of dressed like Gar or at least Bob could never picture Amy wearing a trench coat and ballcap. The only real questions that Bob had was why would either of them be going into a place called Jim Buddies? This looked more like Chuck's kind of hang out. In the end it really did not matter because as Bob walked in the place and up to the front counter, he noticed the sign in book. Thankfully, the last person who signed in was Garcia Alvarez.

Some little brown-haired girl in a leotard and pigtails was working the counter. She was smiling so hard that her freckles looked like they were about to pop off her face. She even winked at Bob as he flashed his badge and then pointed to the back room where all of the weights were, "I got some business here, miss. One of our officers is back there and I need to get him."

It was almost like this girl had a switch that put her head on permanent rocking. Her head never stopped tilting from side to side just like her smile seemed almost chiseled on. She told Bob, "Sure, it's twenty."

"What?" Bob was shocked, "Look I just want to walk back there and get him is all. I promise I won't grow any biceps."

"I don't make the rules," the girl with the bobbing head replied. Bob began grumbling as he fished out his plastic but as he tried to hand it to the girl she pointed to a sign behind the counter. It read, "Deutschemarks Only." Bob went right back to searching his pockets till he was pretty cleaned out of hard currency. There was one last surprise.

The girl pointed to another sign that was over the door to the weight room. It clearly stated, 'Gym Clothes Only.' Bob was horrified, "I don't have any!"

The girl was ready for that. She had already slapped a couple of sealed plastic bags on the counter along with a pair of shoes that Bob figured came right out of a bowling alley. They were sneakers of a sort, but they were also ugly. She was still smiling as she patted them, "Oh. don't worry. Your fee covers all that." She then pointed to a row of makeshift changing rooms that Bob questioned the privacy of. He even bent over and realized that you could see pretty good under the doors that were at best only a collection of slats that missed the floor by a good sixty centimeters.

Bob started to feel pretty self-conscious and he said, "Look, you guys don't like have a bathroom? I'm a little… uh, you know? I don't like changing in public." The girl pointed to another sign that Bob read aloud, "Bathrooms in the back." He then looked at the smiling girl and said, "Don't tell me…"

The girl had a twinkle in her eye, "You have to be changed to go in the back."

Bob gulped as he gathered the bag of clothes and shoes, "How do I know this stuff fits?"

Why was this girl always so damn happy? It was really starting to piss Bob off. She told him, "It all stretches."

With a nasty sneer on his face, Bob entered the dressing room, dumped his shoes, pants, and shirt as he started the bothersome task of getting the sealed bag open. He constantly kept worrying about somebody looking in on him and only then did a more horrifying thought cross his mind. "Where the hell did my clothes go?"

Bob began to panic as he twirled around in the dressing room that had barely enough room to stand in, let alone do anything else. He was hoping that somehow his clothing would just magically reappear but predictably they did not. It took him a second to decide what to do. He had the gym clothes and right now clothing was high on his priority list of needs. Bob finished tearing into the bag and was quite thankful that it really did have clothing inside. His relief was short lived when he discovered that everything that he had was two sizes too small.

Meekly Bob whispered, "Help?"

CHAPTER 15

As the helicopter made a slow and lazy circle of the field, Barbara could not help but notice the very prominent looking aircraft that was still parked in the exact same place that it was when she and Shannon had flown up to their station. Despite the fact that the aircraft was painted camouflage, the big Iron Cross painted on the wings stuck out like a sore thumb. Barbara kind of figured that at least here the Wehrmacht liked sticking out like a sore thumb. It was not like anyone was going to tell them they couldn't do what they wanted to. So why hide?

The only thing different that Barbara could see about the German presence was the activity level around their aircraft. When she had taken off it had almost seemed as if the Germans had just landed here to catch some sleep. They looked pretty busy at the moment. The only good thing that Barbara could say about that was it appeared as if they were getting ready to leave. Barbara could only guess that much because they were not digging holes and setting up big guns so what else could they possibly be doing?

The only thing that looked out of place about the airport was not what Barbara could see but more like what she could not. She set her bird down right in the grassy field that she had taken off from. She even put the skids down on the marks they had left overnight. There was a second set of marks not far from hers and they did not have a chopper sitting on them. After she killed her engine, she sat in her seat to let the blades slow down while she finished turning everything else off. She grumbled to herself, "Where the hell are those two?"

Unfortunately, keeping your volume down with a microphone right next to your lips usually defeats the purpose of doing so in the first place. Shannon, sitting beside her mother, got a big smile on her face and told her mother, "I guess they're out flying the hump, huh?"

Barbara tried to control her temper and she kept her reply short and sweet, "Shut up, Shannon." She then decided to scold her daughter, "It's not funny."

Shannon remained as playful as ever, "Who's joking?"

It was a good thing that the blades were

almost stopped because Barbara decided to just get out now and not answer her daughter. She grabbed her bag from the backseat and did not listen to another word that her daughter had to say as they walked back to the tower. It was when she reached the front door that she froze and gulped. Two grenadiers were standing just outside the door. It was a young girl and boy but with all the equipment they had on it really didn't matter who they were. They both looked intimidating enough. The only good thing that Barbara was relieved to see was at least their battle rifles were slung over their shoulders and they did not appear to be on the lookout for any trouble. She stayed away from the door anyway.

As Barbara debated about what to do another German appeared. He came walking out the door and this guy was big and burly. Barbara got the impression that he would have looked scary without all the military hardware. He had stripes on his sleeves and walked with an air of authority about him. He proved that much when he commanded the other two Germans with only a nod. Barbara held her breath as they walked by. She let it out when they did not even pay her a bit of attention. They simply went their own way, back across the tarmac, to the hangar that their aircraft was parked in front of.

Shannon had been so silent during the encounter that Barbara had almost forgotten she was standing behind her semi hiding. When the Germans were far enough away, ever increasing the gap between them, Shannon stepped out of her mother's shadow and said, "What a bunch of dicks." For once, Barbara decided not to correct her child.

Barbara did not exactly run but she did walk very quickly towards the tower. She was in near panic until she saw Lucy step out and watch the departing soldiers. Lucy looked no worse for wear. She did have a strange expression and if Barbara did not know any better, she would say it was one of surprise and shock. Barbara quickly asked, "Lucy, are you OK?"

"Um," it did seem as if Lucy was at a loss for words. "Yeah, I guess. I'm just…"

"What?" Barbara was very concerned. "What did they do?"

"They paid," Lucy was still stunned. .

Now Barbara was too. She blinked, her jaw fell open, and she asked, "IFOR actually paid for a landing permit?"

"Um," Lucy tried to get her thoughts together and then she said, "not exactly. It was that big guy there, with the stripes. Said his name was... Berg? I think? He rented that hangar they're parked by."

Barbara blinked again, "You're kidding?"

"No, best sale we've made all month. He handed me a wad Deutschemarks and signed a lease." Lucy's eyes were still big, "I hope he don't ever do nothing like that again."

Barbara looked back out towards the Germans and they were still just harmlessly walking away. She finally started breathing normally and with some relief she told Lucy, "I think I need a drink."

Lucy did not even blink, "Already opened a bottle, honey."

Shannon saw the look in her mother's eyes and before the teenager could even get one word out, Barbara just said, "No." They proceeded inside and as Barbara's thought processes began to recover, she asked, "Has Tony checked in? I tried to raise him but couldn't get him."

Lucy was still in shock as she sat down at her little desk and started pouring bourbon into a glass. After handing the glass to Barbara, Lucy just started drinking out of the bottle. After a couple of good swigs, she said, "You'd have better luck in the air than I would down here, sugar. We got limited range here and I can't ever raise anybody up on them slopes. Besides, I didn't figure they'd be back by now anyway."

Shannon crossed her arms, wrinkled her nose, and said to her mother in a snide way, "Told you."

That made Lucy laugh as she commented to Shannon, "That girl sure had some goo-goo eyes. Didn't she?"

"No," Barbara said sternly. Tony might have been a lot of things, irresponsible and self-gratifying being amongst them, but if you put him in a pilot seat he did not take chances. It was something of a contradiction, but it was one that kept him from getting fired. Barbara knew a real pilot when she saw one and she also knew that Tony was even better at it than she was.

Barbara looked to her daughter, "Shannon, stay here and help Lucy out for a

145

while, will you?"

Shannon suddenly switched from good humor to slight fear, "Mom? The Germans? Remember?"

"If they were going to blow this place up, I don't think they would have paid Lucy for the damages in advance," Barbara told her. "Just stay away from them."

Shannon was not very convinced. She then realized the other side of that equation and asked her mother, "Where are you going?"

Now Lucy got it and she put the bottle aside even if her hand did not come off, "That's a really good question, Barbara. I hope you ain't figuring on flying out to the slopes, not on your own, honey. That ain't safe."

Barbara ignored the advice since she was already well aware of it. She remained deep in thought for a moment and then asked, "How are they doing up at," her voice became semi sarcastic, "Loveburg?"

Lucy took another swig and then said, "Killy radioed in a couple of hours ago, right after they landed. They had to ride horses the last few miles on account of them people don't

146

like no planes flying over. He said they was fine but I ain't heard nothing since."

While slipping her sunglasses back on and zipping up her jacket, Barbara said, "When you hear from them again just tell Killian to bring Kent back here. The field up by the station is socked in with snow. I wouldn't try landing a plane on it without a ground team."

"Oh, I see," Lucy nodded as she put the bottle down again. "I was wondering what you was doing back so early." Then Lucy thought about it some more and asked, "Snow? Funny time of year to be getting that much snow even up there."

Barbara walked right out the door without responding. Shannon developed a big grin and she was just about to ask Lucy when she heard her mom yell back from a distance, "I'm checking your breath when I get back, Shannon!"

"Damn it!" Shannon stomped her foot, flopped down in a chair, and commenced to pouting. She then mumbled to herself, "god, Mom's the one that needs to be flying the hump. Maybe she'd lighten up."

Lucy just laughed and took another drink. This time, she put the cork back in the bottle and put it away. She was giggling as she did. Then she said to the kid, "Don't worry, sugar, we're going to have fun. So, tell me I heard you guys got you another one of them treaty fellers. Why ain't he killed himself yet?"

CHAPTER 16

When they had gone to town this morning, Danni had been wondering why everybody in the Arch just did not move out here to Valley. This place seemed so peaceful compared to back on the islands. Danni even entertained the thought of moving here and trying to find a job. It sure beat the hell out of wanting to crawl up in her skin every time she saw a shadow in an alley. She was still dealing with the reactions of having been shot and those were of the kind that nobody ever bothers to mention. They were the kinds of things that made you avoid certain things when you were not even aware you were doing it. It was even worse when you did know.

Of course, the entire debate was settled for her when the first strong gust of cold wind came rolling out of the trees and then hit her. It felt almost like she had been cut in half and that was even while she was still feeling numb from the pain killers. The walking had warmed her right up to the point that she was actually considering shedding a layer of clothing. She did compromise and unzip the flight suit a little. When the wind found its way in the lowered zipper and hit the sweat underneath, Danni gave up the fanciful idea of stripping in the wilderness.

After the shock of the cold wind began to subside, Danni realized that it felt almost like she had been hit in the head with a hammer. She had to stop for a minute and take a knee. Her head was swimming in something but whatever the haze was, Danni couldn't figure. Was this walking? Was it the wind? Could it be the painkiller? The more important question that she had was why hadn't she reached the trees yet? How long had she been walking now? The scary part was that Danni really didn't know. For some reason she had not even cared and for the moment she kind of still didn't. The idea that she was alone in a deserted wilderness was only now starting to occur to her.

Danni got back to her feet and looked back to the chopper. It was sitting up on a small rise across open ground and when Danni compared it to the distance that she had left to go in order to make it to the tree line, she realized that for some strange reason she was only about halfway there. How did that happen? It felt like she had been walking forever! Then Danni started thinking and wondered, "was this the direction that Tony had walked in?" She had remembered thinking that, but now Danni was wondering why? Did she even have a reason for coming this way?

She took another look towards the chopper. Danni felt a sigh of relief. Tony was standing up there. He was looking right at her. Danni waved at him. He raised a rifle to his shoulder. Why would he do that? Where did he get the rifle? That wasn't Tony. Danni panicked and began running away from the gun. She cringed in terror waiting to hear that crack. Her body started feeling sick as it anticipated that pain of hot metal tearing through her flesh.

What came was completely unexpected. It was not the nerve shattering explosion of a bullet leaving its barrel. Danni was too scared to look at first. What she heard sounded more like a swarm of insects. The way it impacted her ears almost tickled when it mixed with the meds. It grew louder but Danni did not look back until the sound had stopped. Even then, Danni might not have checked except she fell just short of the trees. Then she only accidentally caught sight of what was going on behind her. The guy, who still had the rifle, was on a four-wheeler.

She had a better look at the guy now. He was kind of pudgy. He had on hunter's clothes and a ballcap. He probably hadn't shaved in a while and it was pretty easy to tell even from the current distance that the guy had probably not washed his clothes, or himself, in some time. In stark contrast, the big long rifle looked to be in pretty good shape. Why did he want to point it at her? After a few seconds it became quite obvious that this was exactly what he was doing!

Danni felt that fear welling up in her. The guy had only closed about half the distance between the chopper and the trees. He was definitely taking his time to aim. She had a moment to think and she was not going to waste it on wondering why. Danni did not even think she was capable of it anyway and for that matter her brain did not seem to be able to perform any higher functions. She was on her knees in the open with a guy taking aim, and all she could do was nothing! It was like she was frozen in place.

"Danni!"

That was Tony! The voice sounded kind of strange. It sounded almost like he was yelling at her through a funnel. Where was it coming from? Suddenly, with no explanation at all Danni almost completely forgot about the shooter. She got to her feet with no problem at all. She heard her name again and took a couple of steps in that direction. That was when she heard the crack of the rifle. Her body went limp. She dropped and everything went black.

CHAPTER 17

As Norm looked up at the sign, he was starting to get the impression that Jake Barton was taunting him. This place was the next on the list of videos that Jessica Walsh had broadcast from. Jake had even milled around in the background of the video, right next to the barred front window of the business, almost in the exact spot that Norm was now standing. Norm was halfway surprised the guy didn't moon the camera, stick his tongue out or shoot a bird. Now that Norm saw what this place was, an electronics repair shop, he fully understood that Jake did not have to. Given Norm's disability when it came to gadgets, the entire store was Jake's middle finger!

"Sorry, cocksucker," Norm mumbled to himself as he hit the button on his phone that dialed the station. "Tell me I can't use electronics," he mumbled some more until Leslie picked up on the other side of the call. She did not sound so happy either but Norm being Norm simply told her, "I don't care. Where's Cal?"

"Well," Leslie did change to upbeat even if it was still tainted with a tad bit of anger, "He just left to go down to the city jail. It would seem that Amy and Garcia won a lovely getaway for two in the holding tank. Something about, oh, let me see if I remember it all. Um, we have obstruction of justice, illegal concealment of firearms, vandalism of government property, and of course we can't forget a felony car theft charge!" Then she sounded almost confused when she said, "And I still haven't figured out where the contributing to the delinquency of a minor came from. Shannon's not even here!"

Norm took a very good look at his nearby friends while he listened to Leslie. Something was not quite right about them and it revolved around the fact that Norm recognized at least one of them. What made him even more

153

nervous was the fact that one of the three guys in that car was also on a phone. Norm did not like this. The entire setup stank to high hell. He was going to kill Jake if he ever found the asshole!

Norm just put it out of his mind and then asked Leslie, "What about Bob?"

"Oh," Leslie sounded even more perky. "This one I really haven't figured out. His wife called. She wanted to let us know that she would be dropping him off back here at the station, just as soon as she took him his clothes." Leslie paused for a second. It was almost like Norm could hear the girl thinking on the end of the phone. Then she said in a more subdued tone, "Not that him being here will do a lot of good seeing as how all of the station's cars are gone now. They vanished right along with Amy and Garcia."

One of the guys in the car that Norm was watching, was doing something that Norm was not exactly happy about. Norm was starting to get nervous and he was sizing up everybody that he saw. He was also making a mental note of the stores, alleys and any place else that might offer shelter should that become necessary. He wanted to wander back over to where he had parked his car but that was not in the cards for right now.

As Norm kept taking stock of his situation, he did manage to tell Leslie, "Don't you go to worrying about all that. I'll take care of the situation. You just sit your ass right there in ops and do what you're supposed to."

"Yeah," she did not sound convinced and that made Norm wonder if he had been wrong about her this morning. Leslie then put it to him, "Like you handled all that bullshit this morning, Norm? Come on, why don't you tell me what this is really all about?"

"I don't have to tell you nothing, girl," Norm shot back. He then asked, "Speaking of which, who did you tell about that little incident from this morning?"

"Not a soul," Leslie replied with a deep and cutting voice. "And the main reason is I'm not even sure what happened this morning."

"You're doing good, kid," Norm told her in a rushed tone. "Just keep it that way." He hung up the phone as the car that he had been watching pulled out from the curb and began to slowly roll closer. As Norm thought might happen that vehicle was joined by two others that had appeared to just be driving by until they made radical swerves, all at Norm.

Norm took a quick step towards the nearest door. He had his hand in his windbreaker and on his pistol. Fortunately, he did not feel the need to pull it out just yet. None of the passengers of any of the vehicles got out. They were deliberately letting him know this was not an attempt to kill him. Norman eased his hand back out and finally a single car door opened. One man got out and Norm knew him. It was Hyrum Kingsley's main bodyguard, the guy everybody just called Baxter.

The man took his sunglasses off and put them away in his coat. He walked up to Norm as if this was any normal encounter with someone that you knew and happened upon. He stood relaxed with his hands clasped in front of him. Norm recognized a relatively peaceful gesture when he saw it but at the same time, Norm also knew this guy could afford it. Norm counted seven guys with him and there was very little chance that their unseen hands were empty.

Baxter almost sounded bland as he announced, "Mr. Scoggins. My employer wishes to have a few words with you."

Norm acted surprised but in truth he was

even more so than he acted, "He does? Let me ask you this, Baxter. Did Hyrum ever learn how to use a phone? I only ask cause half the time I can't figure mine out for shit."

From Baxter's body language it was quite obvious that he was not amused. He simply stated in a polite but firm tone, "I'm sorry, Mr. Scoggins, did I leave you with the impression that we were asking?"

"Not really," Norm told him. "Unless of course you are, in which case the answer is…" Baxter's quite bland expression did not change a bit. Norm smiled, "I'd love to." Norm then mumbled under his breath, "Jake, if I find you, I'm going to kick your ass." Of all the things that Norm had been expecting from today, this was not one of them.

CHAPTER 18

There was at least one aspect of this setup that impressed Kent. It proved to him that someone had done a little research on the subject that did not include source materials from recreational carnivals or bad movies. The Rennies had their banquet set up with some sort of historical accuracy. The table that he was sitting at beside Jim Dove, was definitely accurate to the fourteenth century style of banquets. Dove was sitting on the highest stool, with Kent just below him. Everybody at the table sat on only one side. It was a detail that movies quite often missed. An army of servants were on the other side, rushing up and down and constantly filling plates and wooden mugs. Kent got the impression that they were all well practiced at this. Dove also mentioned the jousting and tournament games that were scheduled for later in the day. It sounded like they were also practiced at those activities as well.

A quick glance down at Sheriff Rayne and Dr. Dykstra told Kent all that he needed to know on that subject. They both looked rather bored and Kent deduced that was probably because they had seen all this before. They had not been invited to sit at the high table and were making do at one of the many others. Most of those tables were filled with people that lived here even though Kent saw some people that were most obviously not. The differences in dress made such distinctions trivial to deduce.

It also told Kent something else. This was the industry that these people ran here. Were they really running a tourist business? It could not have been that profitable. One of the many requirements of that industry was ease of access. There was nothing about this place that made it easy to get to. If the Rennies decided to put in an airstrip or at the least make a passable road out of the one that Kent had used this morning, then they could quite possibly have a cash cow on their hands. The fact that they did not was also somewhat telling. It meant that their dress, their choice of lifestyles and everything else about them was more than a game to these people. As far as Kent's purposes went, that all spelled out trouble.

Finally, Dove got excited and with a clap of his hands, whatever small amount of authenticity that there was went right out the window. A dance troop of women, mostly younger girls, came parading in past the high table. They were dressed like what most people thought of as belly dancers, but Kent really had his doubts as to the authenticity of the scarce clothing they had on. Kent found himself having to smile politely and nod his approval to Dove, even if he really meant none of it.

As Dove enjoyed the show, Kent leaned over and mentioned to him, "You do realize that this vaccine would benefit your own people the most?"

Dove laughed and slapped Kent on the shoulder. When Kent first learned he would be talking to this man he had pictured Dove as some kind of serious, charismatic, cult leader with a fearsome stare and commanding voice that just oozed short temper. Dove seemed to be none of that. He acted very relaxed and never seemed to have to command anyone. The people here all acted as if they genuinely wished to please the man. Of course, none of this eased Kent's concerns about the situation.

Dove was still smiling when he told Kent, "I can't tell my people to do something they don't want to, Doctor." Dove then thought about it and said, "You are a doctor, right?"

Kent went right on with, "Really, Mr. Dove, it would seem to me that these people are very in tune with your wishes. I would think that a word from you would go a long way towards resolving this situation."

"Not as much as you might think," Dove told him in his usual relaxed way. The guys eyes never left his dancers as he talked, "I guess that's something me and ole Crass have in common. Even if she don't know it."

What was that supposed to mean? Kent was not entirely sure, but the implication of the statement was quite clear to him. Dove considered himself the Governor's equal. Everything that had transpired since Kent's arrival had proven that to him. Dove was acting as if he were receiving a visiting ambassador. It made Kent wonder exactly how true that was. It also gave Kent another idea.

At first, he simply pointed out, "I do believe Dr. Dykstra may have mentioned this, but the simple truth is no matter how much we call this planet home, our species is not from here. Without routine vaccinations we leave ourselves, our entire population, open to infections that medical science has never even dreamed of."

Dove laughed and that was the last thing Kent had expected. Did he not believe what he was just told? Given the surroundings that was entirely possible but then Dove proved otherwise. He was not laughing at what Kent said. He seemed to find the timing as somewhat amusing. Dove pointed out past the dancers, "You mean the same Dykstra that just walked out the door?"

Sure enough as Kent looked, the Valley doctor was at the door to the banquet hall. He took one last look back and Kent could have sworn the man looked disgusted. Then the guy walked out and Kent had to comment, "Strange, I never thought him all that prudish."

Once again, Dove just laughed and then he got a little more serious, "I might be dressed like a reject from Hogwarts but I'm not stupid, Doc. I'm sure you wouldn't be here if you didn't know my background. I'm figuring that's why Crass sent you instead of somebody else."

"Actually," Kent pointed out, "I doubt the Governor even knows that I am the one here."

Dove blew it off, "Whatever, so she thinks that Reilly chick is here, either way she didn't send the Commissioner of Health, she sent Rangers." At that point Dove slipped down off his stool and nudged Kent as he did. Dove nodded to a backdoor, and despite the obvious objections of his honor guard, Dove ignored them and led Kent into a backroom that was obviously some kind of office.

After pouring himself another drink of the mead that had been flowing freely in the banquet hall, Dove then offered Kent a goblet. Kent politely rejected it and Dove snickered, "Suit yourself, Doc. It's one of the perks of this job."

"I see," Kent replied. "Of this job. I take it that your position with these people is just that?"

"Don't get me wrong," Dove told him. "I believe in what we're doing here but as one of the pillars of the community, I do have to be a little more realistic about things." Dove studied Kent and then he asked the Ranger, "I guess you're expecting me to quote you a figure right about now."

Kent found that slightly amusing and he replied, "If money were all that you were after, Mr. Dove, I do not believe that you would have gone to all this trouble. I suspect that what you are really after here is legitimacy. Something that we have already provided you, in some small measure at least."

That drew a wide toothy grin from Dove as he studied Kent out of the corner of his eyes. As he walked towards a comfortable chair he pointed with both hands and said, "I kind of knew that you and me talked the same language."

Kent remained standing and he simply nodded to Dove as he kept things on track, "And this little banquet is providing you with some leverage within your community. I do suspect that what you are after is far more. I'm afraid that when we inform the Governor of this she will not be prepared to go so far."

That made Dove laugh, "What's Crass going to do about it? She can't even keep the Arch in line. She's already got about no authority up here at all. I mean zippo. I'm not really asking for anything here, Doc. I just want her to acknowledge the situation as it really is."

Kent played his next card, "I'm afraid that IFOR might not see the situation quite that way, Mr. Dove."

That drew a hardy laugh from Dove who then waved the notion off, "I can handle the Krauts. That is if they gave a shit about Valley in the first place, and they don't."

With a polite smile, Kent nodded and told the robed man, "Well, I shall convey your message to the Palace. If that is your position, then I really do not see that we have anything more to discuss here."

"Maybe," Dove said in a coy manner, "then again."

Dove stood back up and seemed relatively

serious for the first time since Kent had arrived. Dove went over to his strange looking desk and sat his goblet down. He sat on the corner and crossed his arms as he said, "Course what makes me think this is a really serious matter is I know who you really are."

Kent was about to walk out but now Dove had his full attention. He stopped and played it easy as he asked, "And who is it that you think I am, Mr. Dove?"

Dove simply replied, "Beta Canaan." When Kent did not reply, Dove went on, "Celtlandia? Shanghi Reef? Central Complex? Any of those places ring a bell?" There was still no reply so Dove broke into another big smile and laughed as he said, "Oh come on. You know what I used to do."

Finally, Kent told the man in a polite and friendly fashion, "I don't know what it is exactly that you believe you know about me Mr. Dove, just to say that it is probably not as much as you think."

Again, Dove laughed, "Oh, of that I have no doubt. Let's just say, I know somebody who would be very interested in seeing you again."

CHAPTER 19

As she waited in the car, her eyes kept drifting back over towards the scaffolding and piles of construction material that were stacked up in groups that were each easily larger than anybody's house. Jessica could not help but think about how much of a monumental waste of time and resources that it all was. It was popular in some circles though and for that reason alone Jessica could not touch it with a ten-foot pole. She would love to do nothing but sit down here at the Palace and run stories on government waste and corruption. People's attitudes towards this building, added to the dangerous people it might tick off, made that impossible. It was also not what she was really looking at.

The flowers, the little stands and the blood stains were the things that kept pulling in Jessica's eyes. She could understand the little memorials that people had put up. The real question she had was why had no one gone out there and cleaned up the blood? Jessica knew for a fact that a cleaning crew had worked for weeks on cleaning up the mess from the Family Day attack. Why were there still blood splatters in places? Couldn't anyone do anything about it at all? You could still see stains on some of the walls, the columns and even some of the construction material and they were very obvious.

Another thing that was obvious were the Germans. They had taken their share of casualties in the attacks. The rumor going around was that their commander had actually been the main target. Jessica was not sure if she believed that or not, but the grenadiers sure did. They were in a less than compassionate mood these days. There had always been reports of violence and crime committed by members of IFOR. They would routinely beat people they didn't like or maybe even looked at them the wrong way. They were constantly enforcing rules that stepped on the people who lived here.

It was another story that Jessica could not report on but to a degree she understood it. They were a military garrison and those kinds of problems could usually be expected around any base, particularly one that was little more than an occupation force. Those problems had always been exacerbated by the fact that Earth, all of Earth, had put their official stamp of approval on this and no outside power was willing to step in and help the colony. The Germans simply went unchecked and United

Nations rules guaranteed that every single member of the Wehrmacht was immune from criminal prosecution. Still, those problems were also manageable if for no other reason than the German High Command did keep tight control of their troops. The Family Day Massacre had changed that.

That was why Jessica was somewhat surprised by something else that she saw while sitting in her car. There had been a German soldier who was standing like a statue out in the middle of the park. That was of no great surprise really. You saw them everywhere even if they were never quite so rigid as this guy. Jessica had not even given it two seconds of thought as to why he was there or what he was supposed to be guarding. Everyone around him, both patrons of the park and workers in the Palace, did their best to ignore him. That was also quite normal. Then another set of soldiers approached.

What really looked unusual, to Jessica at least, about this particular group of Germans was how they were walking. Usually, when the Germans went anywhere it was with military precision in nice neat lines and they all seemed to move as if they were being controlled by a single mind. With the exception of the uniforms and all the heavy firepower they had strapped on, this group could have been just an ordinary clump of pedestrians. They approached the guard who made some funny motion with his weapon and then the new arrivals approached a nearby memorial that had just recently been set up. The soldiers then began laying flowers on it. That really stunned Jessica. They actually looked human.

Jessica almost made a squeal of fear when she heard the car door open. She had been so caught up in watching the Germans that she had completely missed Jake. He had tossed whatever he had gotten from the Palace into the back seat of her car and then slid right in next to her. He was on the phone and only half paying attention to her. He then mumbled to Jessie, "Ready? Let's get."

Jessie nudged him and nodded towards a display of sympathy at the memorial. Jake turned, took a glance at it and then shrugged his shoulders. He nodded for her to drive and so she did. Jake went right back to his phone call, "No, do exactly what I told you." Whoever he told that to was apparently not happy about it. After a moment of listening, Jake then said, "I don't know, just go hang out somewhere. I'll call you back in a little bit." He hung up and then asked Jessie, "Where's Norm at?"

Jessica's mind was still back at the Memorial. She had to think on that and said, "Oh, I know he made it as far as the electronics shop. Gary called me and said he showed up. He didn't make it to the pet shop yet." Then Jessica changed the subject by asking, "You didn't think anything about that little display back in the park? You know, the Germans? It doesn't seem to surprise you."

"Why would it?" Jake really did not seem to be surprised. When it appeared that Jessica wanted an explanation, all Jake could say was, "They lost friends. What do you expect?"

"Well if you put it that way," Jessie felt kind of stupid when she looked on it with his eyes. She quickly changed the subject, "You said something about a change of plans?"

Jake settled down in his seat as they reached the next intersection and Jessica waited for directions. He told her, "Yeah, I just got confirmation. I told you about it this morning. I just had to wait till I knew."

Jessica pointed to the left and the right, "Which tells me absolutely nothing."

Jake had to search his pockets for what proved to be a crumpled piece of paper. It had obviously been in his pocket for a while since Jessie had to flatten it out on the steering wheel before she could read it. It was also in very sloppy handwriting and that let Jessie know that Jake did not write this. She decided not to ask and just started driving towards the address on the paper.

Jake then told her, "You can just drop me off at that one. Then you can go back to doing… whatever it is you were doing."

"You mean," Jessie slowed down for a stop signal, "doing all your work for you?"

"Well," Jake amusingly replied, "technically I guess you were doing your job while helping out with mine." With the exception of the first broadcast from the Foo King, they had been following a list of broadcasts that Jessie had gotten from her office and had to make today. As far as Jake was concerned, he needed random and that one was about as random as it could get since he had nothing to do with compiling it.

What Jake did not get was, "You know I don't get it. Why is it that every story you've done today was in front of some business that sounded like you were plugging?"

The light changed and Jessie started driving again. After passing the intersection she said, "That's because plugging is exactly what I was doing." When Jake developed a funny look on his face, Jessica rolled her eyes at him, "Oh come on, Jake. You are not that naive. It's called paying the bills. Product placement? Paying the rent? Buying cat food?" Jake did not answer that, and it appeared as if he was willing to accept the answer. Jessie was the one who was not that settled about it, "Besides, we don't get enough real news stories here. We have to come up with stuff like that."

Jake had accepted all the other stuff without batting an eye. He seemed to accept this as well. That was why Jessie found it strange that she was the one that did not really believe it. Jake also seemed to pick up on that, "Seems to me, there's plenty of stuff going on here."

"Yeah well," Jessie sighed, "not stuff that I can report on. At least, report on and live."

"You got a good point there," Jake said in passing.

Jessie was still the one having a hard time believing it. She then asked Jake, "You wouldn't want me to tell everybody what you're doing, would you?"

"Not particularly," Jake replied. He then added, "Course I wouldn't kill you for it either." They sat in silence for a minute and then Jake suggested, "Why don't you go run a story on that German memorial?"

"Oh," Jessie started out with some serious sarcasm, "what a great idea, Jake." Then she became quite sullen, "And get branded a Nazi sympathizer.
That would really help out my career. Any other suicidal ideas while you're at it?"

"You're right," Jake tossed in his disinterested towel, "I'll let you do your job and I'll stick to mine."

Jessica snickered at that, "That's a really good idea because to be honest I'm not even sure what your job is." When Jake did not respond, Jessica went on, "I mean what is it we're doing? This is not exactly something I ever pictured cops doing."

"Technically speaking," Jake told her, "I'm not a cop, if that clears it up any."

"Ok," Jessica nodded as she sorted through that, "but don't you like, chase bad guys and stuff? Stop criminals? You know?"

173

"Sometimes," Jake replied in a very simple and short tone that spelled out he was not going to give the reporter anymore.

While Jake might have been a professional at not talking, Jessica was a pro at getting people like him to talk. She said one word, "Spy."

Jake laughed but said nothing.

Jessica continued, "Oh come on, Jake. Everybody knows that you treaty guys are just here to spy on us. You said it at the hotel. We're both in the information business."

Again, Jake laughed but this time he did say something, "Spies are in the business of collecting information that other people are trying to hide."

"So," Jessie shrugged.

"So," Jake came right back with, "near as I can tell, nobody is trying to hide anything on this rock. Everybody is pretty brazen about everything."

"Have I ever told you," Jessica said in a sweet and soft tone that quickly soured, "I hate it when you make a point?" She saw the address and then pointed it out to Jake. He then instructed her to pull around the corner where she pulled up to the curb to let him out. Jessica just had to ask, "What are you going to do? Or can I know?"

Jake seemed rather unconcerned about it as he casually replied, "I'm going to steal a car."

Jessica took the news in stride, but she did ask, "I thought you were supposed to stop people from doing that?"

As Jake closed the door he just shrugged and told her, "It's ok. This one is already stolen."

As Jake walked off, Jessica slapped her forehead and closed her eyes as she mumbled, "Why do I always bring in guys like him? Can't one of them ever be normal!" She drove off and went back to work.

CHAPTER 20

"Wake up," were the words that kept

repeating. They sounded sharp, short, and mildly panicked. Then she heard her name, "Come on, Danni, wakeup, girl. Time to go."

Everything snapped into place all at once and Danni could make no sense of anything. She felt like she was being squeezed, choked and entangled. Something very irritating was working its way into her lungs and even after her eyes snapped open, she could see very little. Whatever she was breathing was also getting into her eyes and she had to squint so hard that it hurt. She wanted to rub her eyes clear but couldn't. One hand seemed to be pinned right to her side. The other had very limited range. Something was blocking her elbow and she could not lift her arm as a result.

The only good news as Danni could figure was that despite all of the cold and damp surroundings, she was pressed up against something very hot, "Tony? Oh my god. I thought you were.. I thought I was…"

"Calm down," he told her as his hand gently stroked her cheek and then began clearing away her eyes so she could see. His words sounded so reassuring, "We're ok for the moment, sort of."

Danni realized she was almost

whimpering, and she found that she really didn't care. "Where are we? What's happening?" Her eyes were slowly adjusting. She could see his face in what little light there was. She let out a sigh of relief and laid her head on his chest, "Is this real?"

It was obvious that Tony did not quite understand her meaning because he answered with, "Unfortunately." Danni almost wanted to cry when he said that. She actually liked being this close to him, pressing up against him like this. Then her head started to clear, and she realized that the pressing was because they had no choice. Before she could panic again, Tony calmly asked, "I thought I heard shooting?"

"Oh shit," it all came back very quickly, and Danni took another dip on the emotional roller coaster ride, "There was this guy. He had a rifle! He was…"

Once again Tony's voice was soothing, "Calm down. Danni, panicking isn't going to help. Besides that, I'm pretty sure he's gone. Somebody was poking around up there but I haven't heard it in a while now."

Up there? What the hell did that mean? If there was an up, then that meant there was a down. Were they in a down? Danni was thoroughly confused, "What the hell, Tony?"

"We're in a hole," he calmly told her.

Danni's head snapped up and she tried looking at the one and only source of light. It seemed to be mostly covered over and besides that the dust that was falling made looking in that direction somewhat problematic. Tony had to wipe her eyes clear again. Then Danni had to ask the obvious, "Uh, Tony, how did we get stuck in a hole?"

"Well I was looking for firewood at the base of this tree," he told her. Now he was a little less calm and slightly flustered. There was also an edge of embarrassment in his voice, "It's covered pretty good up there. I kind of stepped in the wrong place."

Danni became furious and started trying to jerk herself free, "I want out!" Again, Tony had to calm her down. She was not doing much more than bringing dirt down on top of them. While it was not enough to risk burying them, since this hole seemed to be mostly comprised of tree roots, it was enough to make breathing difficult. When the little tantrum ended, they were both coughing. Danni finally managed, "Sorry?" She then meekly asked, "Can we climb out?"

"Well," Tony told her, "I was almost out when you dropped in on me."

Danni looked him in the eyes and told him, "Sorry?"

"Not your fault," he told her. "Don't sweat it. We just have to figure out how to get out of here now. There was just enough room for me to climb but, with two of us… I don't know."

Another thought crossed Danni's mind, "What if that guy is still up there waiting on us?"

Tony looked on the bright side, "Well the good news is that the hole is pretty concealed, so he's got about no chance of finding us here."

Danni did not like that there seemed to be an up and downside of this situation, "That means there's bad. What is it?"

Tony took his time and said, "The bad news is that the hole is pretty concealed and nobody else has much of a chance either." Tony knew that somebody would have to get pretty close to the hole in order to hear them. He had heard that guy with the gun poking around up

179

there for at least a couple of hours. He had almost stepped on it more than once and passed them right by. He obviously knew exactly where to look and still could not find it. Barbara would most definitely come looking. She might find the chopper but how would she even know which direction to trek in once she did? It could be days before she could get enough help to actually do a real search!

"I know this much," Tony told her. "No matter if he's up there or not, I don't plan on spending a night down here. Do you?"

"Oh great," Danni sighed, "our choices are being shot or suffocation. What I always wanted!"

"Actually," Tony replied, "I think we stand a much better chance of freezing to death once the sun goes down. If that makes you feel any better."

"I'm just thrilled," Danni told him with the expected amount of sarcasm. Then Danni thought about it for a minute longer. She got tired of rubbing noses with him and just kissed him instead. At first, Tony kissed her right back but then he backed off as much as was possible. Danni backed off to and she told him, "I haven't had the guts to do that."

"What?" Tony was still a little surprised, "You mean except at the print shop back on Family Day?"

Danni winced, "Caught up in the moment?"

"Yeah, well," Tony replied with a heavy sigh, "we're both kind of caught up at the moment right now. I just think we had better spend our energy on getting out of here. You know, right now."

What did he mean by that exactly? Danni understood the obvious but was Tony saying there was an after 'right now' part? Danni kicked her feet as much as the hole would allow. She was now sure there was not much to stand on beneath her. She wiggled against Tony a little more and she tried to pull her arms free again. Then she put her nose to his and said, "Well this is kind of a cliché if you stop and think about it."

"Glad you think so," Tony told her as he used his free hand to shield his eyes as he looked up. "Now we need to get un-wedged. I couldn't do that while you were delirious. You would have just kept falling if I did." After a moment of pulling on a root, Tony then asked, "By the way, you didn't hit your head or anything, did you?"

That question threw Danni off. She thought about it for a second and then said, "I don't think so. I don't have a headache or anything if that's what you mean."

After a grunt from Tony, Danni could feel something along the wall move. She jerked violently and found she had a little more room for her arm. Tony's pulling was causing his body to slide along her's. Danni found it very distracting. Then when he stopped, she had to ask why and he told her, "Well believe it or not, Danni. I mean don't take this wrong way, but you are a little distracting."

Danni perked up, "Really?" She then wanted to kick herself for the outburst and she tried, "Oh, I mean, well, I wouldn't know what you were talking about."

He was obviously unconvinced, "Yeah, right." Tony kept right on pulling and after another chunk of dirt and debris came falling, followed by another round of coughing, Tony happily proclaimed, "I think I'm loose." He started sliding higher and Danni suddenly had enough freedom of range to move both of her arms. That did not come too late either. She had to grab something to keep from falling. One hand found a root. The other found Tony's thigh. He had to stop again, and he told her, "Ok, that's very distracting."

Danni felt embarrassed. She bit her bottom lip and tried to fight back a smile as she meekly replied, "I guess some of us live for distractions, huh?"

CHAPTER 21

The activity that Norm saw as he entered the barbershop almost made him think that the scene was rehearsed. Since Norm was all too aware of what Hyrum Kingsley used this place for, he kind of figured that was exactly what it was. Hyrum was sitting in the chair and the barber was slapping on some aftershave as if he had just finished his task. After Hyrum smiled at Norm, he nodded for the barber to leave. Norm did note that the barber made no attempt to remove the apron from Kingsley. The guy only spun the chair around so that Kingsley was looking at Norm and then he promptly left by the backdoor. Baxter and the rest of Hyrum's goon squad were out front looking right in the windows.

In a cheerful mood, Hyrum said, "Norm, glad you could make it on such short notice."

Norm was not cheerful, "If you brought me here to kill me, Hyrum, I think I don't need to remind you about what I keep in my jacket pocket."

"Oh, come on, Norm," the man said from the chair. "If I was aiming to kill you do you think I'd bring you here to do it? Do you think that I'd be here when it was done?"

Norm nodded and replied, "Then why don't you take that sawed-off shotgun out from under that blanket you wearing?"

Hyrum replied seriously, "I said I wasn't here to kill you. I didn't say I was stupid."

Norm nodded and then told the man, "Fair enough. What do you want, Hyrum?"

"Why," the man went right back to cheerful in an instant, "I want you to come back to work for me. I want to bury the past. I can see a future for you in my organization."

"And I'm not even a Canadian," Norm replied.

"That's always a plus," Kingsley pointed out. Then he went on by saying, "I have a very specific job in mind. Something that you've proven yourself more than capable of. Hell, Norm, you won't even piss anybody off by doing it. Might even make a few folks happy for a change."

"I don't know, Hyrum," Norm told him. "That don't sound too much like my kind of work."

"It's sure better than what you're doing now," Hyrum said in a cheery sort of way.

"I guess with Conner out of the picture," Norm told him point blank, "you've had some room for expansion. Guess you need the extra muscle. Is that it?"

For some reason that seemed to piss Hyrum off. He controlled his temper, but he was most definitely not happy, "Actually I need a few more brains in the outfit. The Legion has got all the muscle it needs. I'm guessing you know what happened to Conner?"

"I got some ideas," Norm told him. Then he mentioned, "What I don't know is how much you had to do with it."

"You know that's not my style," Hyrum said dismissing the notion. "In fact, you know exactly what kind of style it was." So, the old man was holding a grudge after all. Norm kind of figured that might be the case even if Hyrum never had much use for his son. Hyrum confirmed this by saying, "And I don't believe for one second that his wife had the brains to plan something like that."

"You want them dead," Norm just said it. "That about the size of it?"

"Damn straight," Hyrum replied with a very determined look. He then eased up and said, "And my boys been telling me you having some problems with your day job. This treaty feller, he's causing all kinds of a fuss." Hyrum seemed to become genuinely confused for a moment and he said, "Don't rightly see how he hadn't offed himself yet, but stranger things have happened." He then got back on point, "The thing is, I can help you with that if you need it. I can make it all worth your while in a lot of ways. You don't even have to quit your day job if you don't want. What do you say, Norm? For old times' sake?"

When Norm walked out of the barbershop, he eased up a bit. The goon squad began to disperse, and they were obviously not intent on taking him on a short ride to a shallow hole. The only one that approached him was Baxter and Norm just ignored the guy and began walking back to his car. Baxter fell in step right beside him. The guy didn't seem to have too much to say. He simply asked, "How did it go?"

"None of your business," Norm told the man as he stopped at his car door. Then Norm looked at the guy and smiled, "I guess Hyrum don't trust you much, does he, Baxter? That does tell me he ain't quite as stupid as I thought." If Baxter took offense, he did not show it. He was as blank as always behind those sunglasses of his. He was quite emotionless as he reached inside his jacket. Norm looked down at the man's hand and told him, "You looking to lose that arm?"

Baxter slowly removed his hand from his coat and what he produced was not a gun. In fact, it was not anything that Norm had expected. It was just a small portable memory chip, the kind that was pretty common in almost any office. Baxter handed it over and said, "Mr. Kingsley instructed me to give you this. He thinks you will find it most helpful. Now, if you'll excuse me."

Norm looked at it and before the man walked off Norm asked with his usual air of hostility, "What the hell am I supposed to do with this?"

Baxter called back over his shoulder, "Whatever you want."

Norm quickly shot back, "I know that! I mean how does the damn thing work? I don't know how to use this shit!"

Baxter vanished around the corner.

CHAPTER 22

"That is most interesting," Kent said when he heard the news about the Germans. He had noticed that their aircraft was no longer parked at the edge of the tarmac. After he and Killian had parked the airplane and then walked back to the tower, Kent had also noticed that the Germans did not leave any guards behind either. He found it very curious but did not show his true feelings on the matter. All that he had to say after that was, "I suggest that we do not look a gift horse in the mouth."

Lucy was halfway done with her bottle of bourbon. She slapped it on the desk and said, "I'll drink to that."

Killian snatched the bottle away from her, took a swig of it himself and then corked the bottle before putting it away. He then told his sister, "Today it seems that you will drink to anything."

Kent ignored the banter and asked about the two missing choppers. Shannon told him, "Mom went to look for Tony and Danni. I think they're flying the hump." The teen was obviously bored out of her skull and she was not all too happy about being left behind. Kent simply dismissed it as unimportant.

Politely, Kent then turned to Killian and asked, "I wonder if I would be imposing, Sheriff. I would have need of a vehicle for a few hours, if that would not be too much trouble."

For a price it was never any trouble and Kent got the use of an old pickup that normally sat around. It was not exactly Kent's style but then again style was not the point of the exercise. It got him to the San Alamo Bar and Grill which is all that Kent really cared about. Kent found it ironic that the place did not look all that different from many of the buildings up

189

at Jim Dove's settlement. The Bar was constructed of logs and although it had a better roof, the décor was about the only real difference. There was no medieval garb and tapestry here. The place had neon signs and Texas memorabilia plastered everywhere. The few people that were around also had considerably more cowboy hats than Jim Dove's flock.

Kent inquired with a little girl that was tending bar and she pointed him out one of the many backdoors. It led him to the side of the building with a few outdoor tables and big smoking grill. Kent had noticed some white smoke that was rising into the air from that direction when he first arrived. He found one man as the source of that smoke. A silver haired looking fellow, skinny and dressed much like everyone else that Kent had seen so far.

The man never gave any indication that he actually knew Kent was standing there watching him spear slabs of beef with a giant two-pronged fork. He never turned around at all. He just continued to flip the steaks as his scratchy voice mumbled, "Been expecting you. Guess you're a little surprised to see me."

"Not as much as you might think," Kent replied. He simply stood his ground and did not retreat nor walk closer to the man. He then added, "I am a little surprised at the messenger. I can only guess at what a man like Dove would charge you for such a service."

Still watching his steaks, the man replied, "He has his uses, well when he's not a pain the ass. I suspect, that's not what you're really wanting to ask me though." When Kent did not say a word, the man went on, "How's Barbara?"

Now Kent did speak, "Why don't you ask her yourself?"

"I'm busy," the gruff sounding man replied. Finally, the man put down the fork and turned to face Kent. He wiped his hands on a rag and said, "What you really want to know is, why now? That about right?"

"Actually," Kent told him, "I think my first question would be why you're even back here at all. Then I might ask how you did it. Since we both very well know that you won't answer either of those questions, why bother to ask in the first place?"

The man started chuckling as he tossed the rag aside. He was smiling when he said, "Kent Gold. Where the hell did you ever get a name like that from? Sounds a little…”

“Cliché perhaps,” Kent suggested.

“Actually,” the man replied, “I was gonna say stupid. Course, I guess it can’t be any worse than what you’re doing right now. Ain’t it about time you started acting like a grownup again?”

Kent waved the notion off, “I’m done with all of that. You knew that when we parted company.”

Still the man chuckled, “Sure we say that. I might have of even thought that a time or two. We both know it ain’t true.”

Kent decided to return the chuckle, “And now which one of us is depending on clichés?”

He had a very quick answer for that, “Don’t make it any less true.”

“This isn’t the old days,” Kent replied. “Neither of us are exactly young anymore. Whatever you think you’re doing here and now; I seriously doubt if it would be worth the effort.”

That seemed to touch a nerve. The man

was not as easy going as a moment ago, "You have no idea what I'm involved in right now."

"Given our history," Kent replied, "I can guess."

The man went on as if Kent had not even spoken, "You and me both know what they've turned this colony into. Don't tell me you haven't noticed cause I know you're not that stupid."

Kent took the tone in stride and simply replied, "It's not your sentiment that I'm disagreeing with. It's just that I am all too familiar with your methods. I don't see where any good could come of it now."

"Guess we're finished then," the man told him, "ain't we?"

Kent turned to leave but then he stopped and looked back over his shoulder. With a polite smile he did ask, "I don't suppose I'll have any trouble when I start my vehicle, will I?"

The man laughed in such a way to make it clear he did not find it funny. He simply asked in return, "I don't know. Was it made here?"

"Why, yes, it was," Kent told him.

The man snorted and replied, "You should be just fine then, I reckon."

CHAPTER 23

There was some kind of excited and incoherent mumbling that was coming from beneath him. Tony could even feel the vibrations from the sound and then he realized the other sensation was moisture that could only be coming from only one thing. Then Danni stopped talking and used her mouth for another purpose. She bit right into Tony's hip and even past four layers of thick padded clothing. He could still feel her teeth!

Tony slid down just a little and suddenly Danni started coughing. Then, with no small amount of anger he exclaimed, "What did you bite me for!?"

After the coughing died away Danni yelled back with the exact same level of fury, "Cause you were gagging me with your…" She became mildly embarrassed and then yelled again, "I'm not that kind of girl!" After a moment of silence, she qualified her statement more calmly, "Not on the first date anyway."

Suddenly they were both laughing until the dust made them stop. Tony took a moment to rest and catch his breath. Then he told her, "First date, huh? Have to say, Danni, I can sure pick some four star holes, can't I?"

Danni wanted to laugh and cry. Even exhausted like this with her lungs filled with dust, he still made her laugh. She forced out her words since it was hard to speak, "If you start with the jokes about putting your something in a hole, I swear I will bite something more vital next time."

This time as Tony's laughter trailed off, he sounded a little more serious, "I see what the problem is."

Danni's laugh was one of exhaustion, "You mean besides the fact that you're not getting a blow job?"

Tony had to stop and laugh again. He sounded as tired as Danni felt, "No, I'm serious. I mean this hole is almost like a natural trap door. This root up here is working a flap of dirt and grass like it's a spring. Soon as something falls in, it just flips that little plug right back in place."

"I see," which was not a literal truth because Danni could not see much above Tony's waist at the moment. Looking up was also still a problem since every time she tried it dirt was falling in her eyes. There was one thing she was detecting, "Where's the light coming from?"

"That flap isn't as solid as it looks," Tony told her, "unfortunately." Tony began to sound strained and he told her, "I can almost reach it."

Danni tried to look up again and just as she got her head turned the right way, a clump of dirt landed in her face. That negated the question she wanted to ask. She spent the next few minutes trying to recover from that disaster. All that Tony could tell from above was the fact that her face was furiously rubbing up against his flight suit and was she actually spitting?

"Uh," Tony started breathing heavy again, "Danni!"

She snapped back at him, "What!"

"That's making it really hard to concentrate," and that sounded very true coming from Tony's lips. She did as he asked, and Tony was almost sorry about it. He then tried to get himself back on track, "We don't have long. I can tell it's not as light up there now."

Danni just grunted, "So?"

"If we're going to get those filters cleaned, I'd like to do it before dark," Tony told her. He then added, "I kind of don't want to spend the night out here. You know, your friend with the hunting rifle?"

For a moment, Danni just accepted that but as she hung on for dear life while Tony worked above her, a thought crossed her mind, "Wait a minute. You don't have any tools?"

That sounded almost like a setup. Danni was at first infuriated but then found herself strangely complimented. She even found herself just a tad excited. Did he really set her up? Wow! That was kind of romantic and she was going to enjoy every minute of it, after she killed him, of course.

Then Tony did what he was really good at. He stuck his foot in his mouth by saying, "Somebody has to be looking for us by now. That means Barbara's probably already in the area. All we have to do is radio our position and we got tools."

Danni gulped and it had nothing to do with the dust. "Um, Tony?"

He stopped working for a minute to rest again, "What?" Her first couple of tries were muffled again. Tony had to finally be serious and tell her straight up, "Just spit it out and I'm not making a dirty joke."

"I," Danni was being very coy when she said, "kind of broke the radio?" There was no response. There was no movement. There was nothing so Danni meekly asked, "Tony?"

"Nothing, Danni," he said as she could feel him going back to work. "We'll worry about that when we get out of here." He was definitely pulling and digging as hard, as he said, "To be honest, I'm more worried about how I'm going to explain all this to Barbara."

"Why?" Danni was genuinely puzzled. "How can water in the line be your fault?"

He kept right on pushing, pulling, and she could feel his body twisting against hers. He also managed to say, "Cause I got this kind of reputation, you know. I guess after everything with Amy, that's just what people think I'm like." He suddenly stopped, became reflective and told her, "And I'm not."

Danni was even more confused, "You mean, you guys weren't doing it out on your surfboard? Where the hell did all that sand come from?"

"No," Tony sounded almost biting now, "I mean, yes, we were. If that makes you happy, yes. That's exactly what we were doing." He deflated and said, "And did anybody ever stop and wonder why?"

What was there to wonder? He's a guy and she's got pretty red hair. That was all Danni ever figured it was. Now, she was starting to think otherwise, and the sinking feeling suddenly had nothing to do with the hole. Danni mumbled, "You still love her."

Of all the things that he had not heard her say, why was it that Tony picked this instance to have clarity of sound, "Yeah, I guess I do, Danni. I've been asking myself that question for a while and that's just kind of what it keeps coming back to."

Now he was banging away at something with gusto. Danni did her best to shield her face from the falling debris. Finally, it came to a stop and after a few coughs, Danni had to know something, "Why did you break up with her then?"

Tony sounded very surprised at that question, "Is that what she told you?"

"Actually," Danni suddenly realized something, "she didn't tell me anything. I just.. You know? It kind of figured."

The only answer that Danni got was Tony going back to work and this time the result was a sudden flood of light. Tony sounded relieved now, "I can get out. Hang on to something." He wasn't kidding either. His body slipped up past the tangled roots with an ease that Danni had almost come to think impossible. She also found herself covered with more dirt and debris than at any point since she got stuck down in the hole. She had not been ready for the one-two punch.

Tony had very little time to celebrate the victory. He had his own one-two punch of sensations to deal with. His body was overreacting to the sudden freedom while the sweat and mud that covered most of this clothing and skin felt like they were instantly freezing in the cold air. Tony had thought it was cold down in that hole, but the reality was it had been rather warm compared to the surface.

It took him a second to realize that he had kicked a lot of dirt loose and that all of it fell right back in the hole. It was not very much, at least not when you were standing around on the ground. That hole was not all that big though. Down below for Danni it must have seemed like an avalanche. Tony heard her screaming while something crashed down there. He quickly spun around on his belly and looked back down in the hole.

After yelling her name, a couple of times, Danni finally replied with some more coughing, "I'm here. Tony, I-uh, think I'm stuck again."

A smile grew on his lips and Tony collapsed on the spot. He breathed a sigh of relief and then finally he told her, "It's ok, Danni. I got out. We do have rope up in the chopper. I got some at the hardware store. I'll go get it, lower it down, and we can get you out easy."

Danni did not sound entirely sure of his plan, "Um, ok. Just, you're not going to take that long are you?"

Tony pushed himself to his feet and told

her the stupidest thing he had ever said in his life, "Just stay right here. I'll be right back." If she said any angry words to him then Tony figured he had kind of earned it. He did not care. If he had to take shit from her for the next year, then that was good. It meant they would both be alive. That's all he cared about at the moment.

He ran out into the field and came to a sudden stop when he saw what was sitting up on the little ridge where his bird was parked. There was another chopper sitting not far from it. Even better was the fact that Tony knew that other chopper. It was Barbara's! They'd already been found! Things were getting even better now! From that point, Tony ran right up the hill to his chopper without even realizing he had done it. When he reached his bird, he noticed that the engine covers were off. The fuel lines were detached as well. Even the back-compartment spaces were open and an air hose was plugged in to the compressor. He almost tripped over the air wrench that was attached to the other end of the hose and just lying around on the ground.

That all looked good to Tony's eyes, until he asked a very relevant question. Where the hell was Barbara? Then Tony remembered that there was a homicidal maniac running around on the loose. Everything looked to be just abandoned in place. Did Barbara have a run in with this guy? Tony started to panic all over again. He cupped his hands over his mouth and yelled out her name.

The answer came from right behind him and it was quite hostile, "You have a lot of explaining to do."

Tony screamed, spun around and really tripped over the air wrench this time falling flat on his ass. Then from the ground, he snapped at Barbara, "Don't do that!"

Barbara sat the fuel filter down and then grabbed a rag from her back pocket. She watched Tony get to his feet and studied him closely. It was hard to miss all the mud, dirt, and grime that she could not even begin to identify. She also softened her tone, "What the hell happened to you two?" Suddenly Barbara was a little concerned, "Where's Danni? Tony?"

Tony started stumbling for words, "It's a long story, I mean, it got long when I was looking for wood and then I kind of got stuck in Danni's hole and I had to pound away at..." Tony went to a knee, almost collapsed from exhaustion and then looked at the horrified expression on Barbara's face. He finally managed a coherent sentence, "That didn't come out right."

Barbara crossed her arms and huffed, "You had best explain yourself."

"Danni," Tony got out between heavy breaths of both panic and exhaustion.

"Yes, I got that part, Tony."

"She's stuck in a hole," Tony finally told her as he pointed back towards the tree line.

This was not a story that Barbara would have expected had it been anything but true. She reached into the open back door of her chopper and pulled out a canteen that she quickly tossed to Tony. Then as he drank, she quickly checked him for obvious signs of injuries and trauma.

As soon as the canteen was emptied, and it took no time at all, Tony was ready to go back and get Danni. He brushed off Barbara's examination. He also felt more coherent now, "She's still down there. We're wasting time. I'm fine." Then Tony looked up at the engine compartment and back down at the filter. It was one of several and as he very well knew, it was also the biggest, "How did you get that down by yourself? I know it's possible but…"

"I didn't," Barbara said as she reached in the storage compartment and grabbed some rope, "I had help."

Tony wondered and then asked, "Did Kent fly out here with you? Where is he? I thought…"

A portly man with a scruffy looking face came walking around the chopper with one of the filters in his hand. Tony had never seen anyone else out here, but Danni had described her attacker well enough. They had plenty of time down in the hole to talk about a lot of things and that had to be the single biggest topic. Tony really thought that the chances of two people walking around way out here and dressed pretty much the same, were virtually nil. What was even more important was that Tony saw the rifle slung on his shoulder and the look on the guy's face when their eyes met.

The man went for his rifle and Tony went for the gun that was always strapped under his pilot's seat. Unfortunately, Tony discovered the gun was also another of the items that Chuck had removed. Tony was swearing as the pudgy guy leveled his hunting rifle and said, "You're that douche bag that fell in the hole. How did you get out?"

Barbara raised her hands as if she were telling them both to stop. She was also a bit confused, "Everybody just calm down, here. What the hell is going on?"

"Barbara," Tony said in a semi-rage, "this guy tried to shoot us earlier."

"What?" Barbara was even more confused now. She looked at the guy's leveled rifle and her hands went up a little higher as she realized the guy was serious. She asked him, "Why would you do that?"

Tony had an edge in his voice as he asked his question, "And then turn around and help her?"

The man was practically snarling now, "You're here to jump my claim. Just like those damn gorillas that Benthic sent out here. Who sent you? Was it Benthic? How much do they know?"

Barbara tried to be rational, "Mister, look. It's like I told you. We're Rangers. We just flew up here from the Arch to deliver some drugs."

The man laughed in her face, "Tell another one, lady. They disbanded the Rangers a long time ago."

Tony slapped his forehead, "Oh god, not that again."

Barbara remained steady as she told him, "It's the truth. You can see we had some mechanical trouble. That's all. Nobody wants your claim."

"Bullshit," he was not convinced.

Barbara played a hunch, "Well I guess if you don't believe us, you're just going to have to kill us."

The man steadied his rifled on his shoulder, pointed the barrel at her head. His eyes narrowed in on the sight as he told her, "Guess I am."

Tony flinched at the sound of the gun.

CHAPTER 24

The angry shouts were quite frantic until

Jake walked in the screen door. Then the commissary exploded with even more anger as Jake stopped in front of the tables and faced everyone else. Norm slipped in right after that, but he stayed as far out of the way as possible. He had even given Jake the few seconds lead because he wanted to make sure if bullets started flying then he would still be outside and near adequate cover. Fortunately, all anyone did was yell at Jake.

Jake's voice raised above all the others and he angrily tossed it right back in their faces, "Are we done?" The shouting slowly trailed off to a few angered rumbles before Jake told everyone, "Good. Now you're all pissed at me. That's fine and you'll get over it. In fact, I'll give you a chance to get over it. Anybody that wants to kick my ass, you have my permission to try."

Jake looked at the eyes that were looking back at him. He was really hoping one of them would try. It was not because he wanted to hurt anybody, and Jake was pretty sure he could take anybody in the room but what he was really hoping to see was that fire, some anger, someone with guts. Calvin sure didn't have it but then again, he got off easy today. Jake had suspected that Garcia might do something, but the guy just looked away and sat there. Jake did find that Amy was looking at him. Her eyes were scornful, and she would not break contact, but she was only thinking and none of those thoughts were about violence. Jake didn't even bother to read Bob.

The only person in the room that was even considering it appeared to be Leslie and she had the least reason to try. Maybe that was why she did nothing but sit on the back counter and grin. No, Jake thought, she was not making a move because she estimated that her chances of taking him down were not good. Besides that, she also seemed to be only interested in trying for fun. Jake figured he was safe there too.

"Since nobody wants to try," Jake told them.

Cal spoke up for everybody who nodded as he told Jake, "We just want to know what the hell is going on?" Calvin looked to Norman, "Why did you want us to follow Jake?" Then he looked back to Jake, "And did you have anything to do with what happened to Amy and Gar? What about Bob?"

Jake remained stern, "I am taking it from your question that you didn't tell anybody about what you had to do to get Amy and Garcia out of the lockup."

"How would you?" Calvin suddenly realized he had the answer to his question and did not care to confirm anything else, "I have no clue what you're talking about."

Garcia mumbled, "That's a story I got to hear." Then he spoke up a little louder and with an edge of anger, "And I bet it has something to do with a little freckle-faced brunette named Betsy."

"As a matter of fact, it did," Jake told them point blank. "Her name is Betsy Fry. She's a twenty-two-year-old farm girl from Iowa." In reality, she was from Chicago, but Iowa sounded better.

Then Bob asked, "What's an Iowa?"

So much for that. Jake also did not bother to tell them that she was a corporal in the US Marine Corps. "This little girl out-smarted every single one of you. Yeah, I gave her the basic guidelines, but I left the details entirely up to her. She waved red flags in front your faces, one after the other. None of you saw it. You just kept right on and that's why every last one of you failed, miserably."

Leslie was still perky and she pointed out

from the back of the room, "Except for me."

Jake snarled at her, "You got lucky. That's all."

Amy was still fuming when she asked, "Why would you do this to us?"

"Oh," Jake singled her out with a point. "Are you pissed, Agent Hiller? GOOD!" It was not only Amy who flinched when he said that. Then Jake asked, "If you're that mad then why don't you come up here and kick my ass? Right now!" There was nothing that followed but silence.

Jake watched heads bow and then he said, "This was a training exercise. You may be pissed at me now, but I don't care. I would rather you be pissed at me and alive than dead just because I'm as lousy at doing my job as all of you are at yours. Agent Nguyen already had to pay that price. Next time we might not be so lucky. Next time it'll be a coffin and a flag and how many of our friends do we want to bury? Cause in case you haven't figured it out, if you fuck up with the people we're playing with it won't be a fatal embarrassment, it'll be just plain fatal."

In contrast to everyone else, Calvin was

only half cowering in his seat instead of all the way. That was why he was the one to ask, "So was there an actual point to all this?"

"Yeah," Jake sternly replied. "That it's time to pull your head out of your ass. Everybody." Jake then pulled a set of keys out his pocket and tossed them to Bob, "Your car's parked outside." He then walked out the door and slammed it behind him.

The room erupted into angered shouts once more. This time they were directed at Norm who was still standing by the door with his arms crossed. He just shrugged at the accusations being thrown his way and he told them, "If I was you people, I wouldn't be worrying about what it is me and Jake been doing. That coffin he was just talking about; it might be yours." Norm left by the same door as Jake.

Leslie happily slid down off her counter and was practically skipping back towards the stairs. She made a sly comment for all to hear. The cocky attitude was just oozing from her lips, "I knew it was all bullshit. Night, gang."

When Leslie was gone Amy sneered and then mumbled, "Bitch."

In the parking lot, Norm stopped next to the station's cars and leaned up against the closest one. He watched Jake who was just watching the station and listening to the commotion that was still clearly audible way out here. Norm dropped his head, shook it and then told Jake, "You damn lucky they didn't shoot your ass. For that matter, you damn lucky they didn't shoot me too. Cause I done told you, Jake, you get my ass killed and I'm taking you with me."

Jake did not respond so Norman pointed out, "You know, it might have gone down a little better if we'd told them the whole story."

Now Jake did speak, and his voice was calm and very sure, "They're not ready yet." Then Jake had a light bulb go off in his head. He reached into the back of a station car and retrieved a hand full of folders that he tossed to Norm, "Take them home and add them to your garage collection. I had 'em printed out cause I know how much you love electronics. Guess you can tell Darcy they're her grandmother's good china or something."

Norm flipped through the tabs on the folders and quickly saw the pattern, "Where the hell did you get these, Jake? These are our goddamn personnel files."

"What?" Jake just shrugged, "I'm the boss and I'm not supposed to have the files on my own people?"

Norm sighed, "Yeah, you the boss till Barbara gets back and then she's going to have a nuclear meltdown when she finds out you been poking around in her office."

Jake's eyes were still focused on the light of the screen door. There was still quite a bit of yelling going on in there. He did tell Norm though, "Don't ask where I got 'em."

"You on your own with this one, Jake," Norm told him but tossed them in his car window anyway. He then asked Jake, "Did we get what we were really after today?"

Now Jake looked at him, "Sure did, and I think then some. We had to ad lib our way through some of it, but I think the plan worked like a charm. We managed to spread them out pretty thin."

"It might be a moot point," Norm told him. "I think I already know who they are."

"If you mean Kingsley's guys," it was obvious that Jake was not entirely convinced, "they're just a part of this equation."

Norm put his hands on his hips and asked, "Now how the fuck did you know about that?"

"What did he ask you for, Norm?" Jake shot back with. "Don't tell me, he thinks we had a falling out and he wants you to kill me or something like that."

"As much bullshit as you got me in, Jake," Norm replied in a very serious manner, "Hyrum don't need to pay me anything to kill you. Just for the record though, no, that wasn't what he wanted."

"Oh well," Jake nodded in return, "too bad. Might have been interesting."

As Norm walked to the driver's side of his car, he added one last thought, "No, what's going to be interesting is you trying to sleep here tonight." After opening his car door Norm gave a great big huge smile and then left without another word.

CHAPTER 25

Not that Jake had taken Norm's idea all that seriously, but Jake was kind of glad that he woke up and nothing had happened. Norm might have understood the streets, but Jake's skill set was of an entirely different nature and there were things that Jake did not even tell Norm. It was not because there was any specific reason for keeping these things a secret. It was more like telling the man would just be a waste of time. Norm just wouldn't care. Some of these things were the reason that Jake had known he could get away with certain things now. What he was doing, well most everything he was doing, was not of an arbitrary nature and the timing of these matters were sometimes critical.

The people at this station knew him now. Most of them trusted him to a degree. Some even respected him. They had taken some pretty hard blows and survived. They had also slid a bona-fide win under their belt. To Jake, this was all currency that had to be spent wisely. Jake was not even sure if Norm understood the scope of things that were most likely on the way. If they were not ready then people were going to start dying and that was something Jake did not want to see happen, ever.

After Jake turned the shower off, he just stood there for a minute. He listened to a very quiet station and that was really the problem. It was way too quiet. That could mean all kinds of things and by Jake's estimation none of them were particularly good. He could locate one person though.

This person was just standing there on a tiled floor and would shift weight from one foot to the other every now and then. This person was trying to be quiet. Jake reached up into the I-Beams that supported the ceiling where they formed a little cubby hole. He put his hand on the plastic bag that was hidden there. He waited a moment as he heard the person lean up against a sink. No, this person was not here to do anything violent or at least not deadly. If it was a bad guy they would have already walked in here and tried to kill him. Jake left the bag with the gun in its hiding spot.

This situation required an entirely different kind of strategy. Jake walked out of the showers, with his towel on his shoulder and nothing else. As he casually strolled over to the sinks and his bathroom bag, he asked the person leaning there, "When did you get back?"

Barbara crossed her arms and pretended that Jake actually had clothes on, "Enough time to get an earful."

So that's why the station was quiet. Everybody was outside waiting to ambush Barbara before she got in the door. Jake almost laughed but he did not want her to think he was making fun of them, so he remained casual but humor free, "So how did your little vacation go?"

Barbara was not in an amused frame of mind. Jake could not quite blame her really. She had just finished a very long flight and to be here now meant that they had left Valley Point pretty early. Barbara sure sounded it as she said, "Well let me see." Barbara was trying to concentrate as Jake began shaving, "the long and the short of…" She stopped and rephrased her words, "Tony crashed a chopper, Danni got stuck in a hole, Kent was the guest of honor at a medieval banquet, and some old prospector tried to kill me."

Jake stopped shaving for a second. He looked at Barbara in a very serious way and then asked, "Medieval banquet? What the hell is that supposed to mean?"

Barbara was even less amused, "Really funny, Barton."

"You ok?" he went back to shaving.

"Yeah," she said with no enthusiasm, "Danni snuck up behind him and shot the guy."

That did alarm Jake. He sighed heavily and asked with his head bowed, "Did she kill him?"

"No," Barbara said in an almost business-like fashion. "She put a hole in one cheek and it went right out the other. Fortunately for this guy, he had plenty of ass to spare." Then she waved the entire matter off, "We turned him over to the sheriff and came on back. I had enough of Valley for the week. Course, I'm not sure I wasn't the lucky one."

Jake was now chuckling about the prospector. He just had to say it, "Maybe for punishment they'll sentence him to the chair."

Barbara ignored him and went on, "What in the hell were you doing to my station while I was gone? You stole our cars. You abused our people. You..."

Jake's head snapped up, "Did you say what I thought you said? Was there a plural possessive pronoun in there somewhere?"

"I have tolerated these little shenanigans," Barbara went on, "that you and Norm have cooked up but this time you went a little too far."

"We're being watched, Barbara," Jake told her in a calm way as he kept right on shaving.

"What?" Barbara felt a chill run up her spine, "By who?"

"That's what we're working on," Jake said with a shrug and then he started cleaning out his razor.

Barbara was still alarmed, "How long have you known this?"

"Oh, I don't know, let me see," Jake pretended to think about it and then he just spit it out, "Since day one maybe?" When she didn't reply he told her, "Oh come on, Barbara. Whoever these people are, they seem to know every little thing we're doing. They knew right when and where to hit us. We are not dealing with the kind of people who do things on a whim. The stuff they're doing takes planning and that requires intelligence. How are they getting that?"

Barbara settled down and became very serious, "Ok, Barton, I'm game. How?"

Now Jake became slightly disturbed, "I don't know, that's what we're trying to find out."

Now Barbara was thinking about everything she knew. She asked with genuine curiosity, "And the whole training exercise thing? That was just… an excuse?"

"Naa," Jake shook it off and began gathering his things. "It was real enough. Nobody said we couldn't do both at the same time."

"Ok, Barton," Barbara shook her head in disbelief, "I don't get it but I also…"

After Jake rubbed his chin off with his towel, he then tossed it back over his shoulder and walked right up to Barbara. She almost took a step back but forced herself not to. Jake squared off with her and told her, "The kind of people we're dealing with, they don't do anything for one specific reason. Anytime they make a move, they got all kinds of things they want accomplished. That way if one goal fails, several others succeed and they're still ahead of the game. It also serves as camouflage. If you don't know the whole plan, and they make sure very few people actually do, then whatever any outsiders see just look to be a series of random events."

Barbara's breathing was a little bit heavier than normal, "And that's what you're seeing here?"

Jake just shrugged, "It's black bag one oh one, Barbara. These guys learned the same playbook I did and if we're going to take them down then we have to play it the same way."

"And how did this mess you made help with…"

Jake ticked it off, "We spread the cars out. One was at the city impound lot and I had the other one parked in view of a security camera that was owned by a business I had access to. We spread our people out and separated them from the cars. We made it look like we had an internal rift, what the spooks call a mole hunt. That way they thought we were divided."

Barbara nodded, "You were sending them the picture you wanted them to see."

"Exactly," Jake nodded and then

continued, "And we hit them with it so fast that they had to tax their resources to keep up. That means they would most likely make a few mistakes. Meanwhile I swapped cars with one that they thought was out of the game and did my own surveillance."

Barbara's eyes got big and she was slightly irked, "Did it work?"

Again, Jake just shrugged and remained cool. He walked past her and as he did, he told her, "Remains to be seen. We're working on it."

Now Barbara was truly frustrated. She practically grunted at Barton as he walked out the door, "So what next?"

He stopped, looked back at her and then said, "Well that's the bad news. We tipped our hand. Now, they know we know. Yesterday, well that was our first real offensive in this little war. It was just a scouting mission, but we made them react to us for a change. They're going to remember it and they are not going to be happy." Jake walked back to his room.

THEY were not the only ones who were unhappy. Barbara snorted in fury and then walked back to her own room. She had to admit that there were certain parts of Barton's logic that made sense. At the same time, the rest of it seemed entirely insane. Barbara was not sure which infuriated her the most, when Barton was wrong or when he happened to be right.

Then there was just that little sneaking suspicion in the back of Barbara's mind. She could not get past all of the things that Idhitri had told her about Barton. She could not get past his keeping secrets from her, his little vanishing acts, all of it was very suspicious to her. No matter what Jake Barton did, no matter how many times he might be right, when you boiled it all down there was only one real thing that mattered. He was not one of them. For that reason alone, Barbara had a very hard time trusting the man, even if she had no real proof that he was anything but what he said.

Barbara stopped in front of her door and put down her things. She grabbed the combination lock that she had recently started using. When she went to enter the combination, the bottom part slid right off the bar before she could even turn the dial. It not only unlocked but it separated completely in two. Someone had not only broken her lock, but they did it in a way that showed no damage at all, then put it back. Why would anyone do that?

The answer was very simple. Only one

person at this station had those kinds of skills and more important, had a reason to do it. Barbara gritted her teeth and in a very guttural roll she said his name, "Barton!"

TO BE CONTINUED